# *Felipe moved one hand and tilted her face*

"You are afraid to be a woman."

"I'm not afraid of anything!" Maggie assured him, struggling back into her old character almost frantically.

"You are afraid of me." He looked down at her steadily, and Maggie tried to stay cool, but she was losing this battle and she knew it.

"I'm not!" Even to her own ears the denial sounded weak, and he smiled grimly.

"We will see."

Dear Reader,

We know from your letters that many of you enjoy traveling to foreign locations—especially from the comfort of your favorite chair. Well, sit back, put your feet up and let Harlequin Presents take you on a yearlong tour of Europe. **Postcards from Europe** will feature a special title every month set in one of your favorite European countries, written by one of your favorite Harlequin Presents authors. This month we invite you to visit Andalucía, the southern region of Spain. It's a place of sunshine and sand, of snow-peaked mountains and sleepy villages. It's a most fitting setting for Maggie and Felipe's love story.

The Editors

P.S. Don't miss the fascinating facts we've compiled about Spain. You'll find them at the end of the story.

## HARLEQUIN PRESENTS

### Postcards from Europe

# PATRICIA WILSON

## Dark Sunlight

# Harlequin Books

TORONTO • NEW YORK • LONDON
AMSTERDAM • PARIS • SYDNEY • HAMBURG
STOCKHOLM • ATHENS • TOKYO • MILAN
MADRID • WARSAW • BUDAPEST • AUCKLAND

ISBN 0-373-11644-6

DARK SUNLIGHT

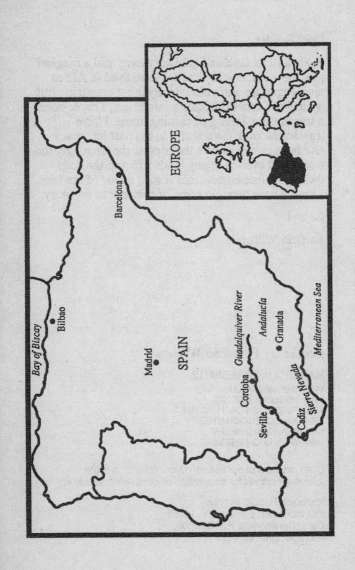

Dear Reader,

Spain and its fascinating history have held a magical lure for me since childhood. I have lived in Africa and Singapore and visited many other countries, but whenever I cross the border into Spain, I experience a tremendous feeling of coming home. I have traveled all over the country in the past few years and have grown to love the people, the language, the wonderful ever-changing landscape and the deep feeling of timelessness that is such a part of the land. I hope I have brought some of this love to my story.

Enjoy!

Patricia Wilson

## Books by Patricia Wilson

HARLEQUIN PRESENTS

# CHAPTER ONE

LATE three times in a row! Maggie tapped her hand impatiently on the steering-wheel and inched slowly forward. She had ten minutes to get out of this jam, park and make it to the office. Monday had been excusable, the roadworks unexpected; by Tuesday the roadworks had grown and even though she had set off earlier she was still late. Today she looked like being later than ever and the excuse was beginning to look a bit thin. Richie would snarl at her. She shrugged her slender shoulders and submitted to fate. She would snarl back after all, so why worry?

A glance at her watch as she turned to the car park told her she was not doing too badly after all. If there was a space she might even be on time. She leaned across and took her ticket, the cold rush of air as she wound down her window making her shiver, in spite of her warm suit. April and it was still like this. It seemed that winter would never go.

She wound up the window and started to cruise round, her eyes searching for the nice little space that would take her white Golf GTI. She saw a place at the end of the row and accelerated thankfully. Three minutes to spare. If she strode out she would just about do it; her office was only across the road and down the side-street.

A bright red Porsche came in from the wrong end, ignoring the arrows and signs. He was coming so fast that she knew he had not seen her and she had to brake sharply, frowning with exasperation. It would be a man, of course; only a man would have the sheer effrontery to do that.

Her frown changed to open-mouthed astonishment,

her exasperation to rage as he drove slickly into the space—*her* space, and Maggie reacted completely in character. She was out of the car at once, the door slammed, her aggressive, slender height bristling with rage as she advanced on the Porsche driver. He was just getting out of the car and he could just get back in it and move out with the same expertise.

'This is *my* parking place!'

He was bent in the act of locking the car as Maggie came up and he straightened to a considerable height, dark eyes running over her in astonishment. Men, their height, their masculine authority, never bothered Maggie. She was not even bothered by glittering black eyes, and her own clear grey eyes met his indignantly.

He stood perfectly still, studying her coolly. She was wearing a smart, oatmeal-coloured trouser-suit, the trousers pushed into high leather boots. Her hair was hardly showing at all because it was also crammed out of sight beneath a very masculine hat that matched her suit.

'Did you hear what I said? You came in like a maniac, moving against the flow of traffic, and you've taken my place!'

'I heard you,' he informed her icily, one black brow raised coldly. 'I would have to be deaf to ignore your voice.'

'Then, as you're not deaf, kindly reverse and go. This is my place and you're in it!'

Maggie glared at him but he bent again and locked the Porsche, pocketing the key and shrugging into a thick leather jacket. He was going to ignore her! If he hadn't been at least six feet two, Maggie would have hit him. He simply moved out from between the cars as if he was going to walk off and Maggie took two aggressive steps forward.

'Abandon the idea,' he warned quietly. 'I would not take kindly to it.'

Evidently he had read her fleeting thoughts of

violence and Maggie stopped dead, her cheeks flushing with annoyance and a certain amount of embarrassment.

'Yes,' she snapped. 'I can well imagine that somebody like you would strike a woman. If I were a man you wouldn't dare do this!'

'But I thought you *were* a man.' He looked her over with sardonic surprise, his carved lips quirking sceptically. 'Your clothes and your attitude are surely less than feminine. You must forgive my mistake.'

'Very amusing!' Maggie raged. 'I'm glad you're enjoying this. Your chauvinistic behaviour has made me late. I never expect to meet a decent man but you take first prize as a pig.'

'Let me know when the prize is to be collected,' he said sarcastically. 'Meanwhile, I'm sure you will be able to bully your way into another place. Look for some old gentleman.'

He just walked away and Maggie lost further minutes staring after him with murder running through her mind. Tall, broad-shouldered and moving like a great dark cat, he infuriated her, confirming yet again her opinion of men. He was staggeringly handsome, a cold masculine beauty about him, with high cheekbones and a hard, compelling mouth.

With a face like that he would naturally be constantly above himself, and he wasn't English, that was for sure. He was too dark, his hair midnight-black like his eyes, his skin too dark to be merely tanned. He was handsome in an altogether splendid way and probably knew it by the haughty way he behaved. There had been some sort of slight accent too. A foreigner, taking *her* space in a car park in London!

'What's the world coming to, eh?' The attendant sauntered up and grinned at Maggie. 'Can't stay here, though, Miss Howard. Late again, are you?'

'I wasn't,' Maggie said irritably. 'What with the roadworks and then this maniac. . .'

'There's a little place in the next row,' he informed

her soothingly, still smirking. 'I'll keep it for you until you drive round.'

Maggie went back to her car and continued to fume. If she had been a man she would not have had to drive round, she would have simply gone the wrong way and got there sooner. And why hadn't the attendant come and told the foreign autocrat off for coming in the wrong way? Obviously he had been listening to the battle. It was because he was a man too, she concluded. They stuck together, presenting a united front to the world.

By the time she had parked she was twenty minutes late and quite beyond caring. She stalked off across the road, her hat jammed firmly on her head and her mouth set in a mutinous line. A perfect way to begin her day. She knew exactly what was meant by manpower!

Maggie pushed her way through the swinging plate-glass doors and as usual the first thing she saw was a giant mock-up of the front of the magazine, glossy, colourful and slightly daunting, the name magnified out of proportion: *QUERY*!

It was a greatly respected and slightly feared publication, dealing in hard fact, abrasive as Maggie herself was abrasive. She had been a feature writer here for two years and at twenty-five she had already made a name for herself. The world of the Press knew Maggie Howard, and hardened newsmen tended to duck although they looked every month for her byline and read her features avidly.

Hard facts were her business. If Maggie said a thing was so, then it was. She had never found any place in the world intimidating when she was after a story and she had the ability to ferret out facts, an uncanny instinct for the truth. She worked with one photographer, some of the shots he had brought back spectacular, and he was waiting for her as she walked into the office.

He pointed at the clock as Maggie went to her desk and put her bag down.

'Nearly twenty-five minutes late,' Bruce Mitchell reminded her hurriedly. 'Don't hang about, Maggie, the boss wants us.'

'Men!' Maggie glared at him and took off her hat, shaking her head to free the mane of dark red hair that cascaded to her shoulders. Mahogany, gleaming and slightly wavy, it caught the light with minute flecks of gold.

'What do you mean — men? I'm a man!' He looked at her indignantly and Maggie grimaced.

'Not you, Mitch. I forgave you for being a man ages ago but, generally speaking, the male sex is. . .'

'Don't say any more,' Mitch laughed. 'You'll think of a good word when you've seen Richie. He's been waiting for the past half-hour.'

'More fool him,' Maggie muttered, sliding out of her jacket. 'I'm only twenty-five minutes late.'

'He came in early to get us,' Mitch informed her. 'It seems he has orders from above.'

'Believe me,' Maggie snapped sarcastically, 'no deity would own him. His language makes my hair stand on end.' She tucked in her brown silk blouse, tossed her red hair free and strode off towards the editor's office, Mitch behind her admiring her slender figure and keeping his thoughts strictly to himself. Nobody but nobody commented on Maggie's shapely form — not unless they wanted acid dripping on them from that sharp tongue.

He grinned, glad she couldn't see him. It was a privilege to work with Maggie Howard. She was wonderful at her job and utterly unaware that she was fabulous to look at — tall, slim, with a skin like magnolia blossom and astonishing hair. There was something about her that was sensuous, all the more so because she had no idea about it. Beneath that hard exterior was a smouldering innocence that every man in their sphere saw and wanted. The trouble was, they did not have the nerve to act. Maggie could kill at sixty paces with one look.

Richie Lowell glanced up as they came into his office and then pushed his spectacles up into his greying hair. His eyes flared over Maggie as he nodded her to a seat.

'I'll not mention the fact that you're late again,' he growled.

'Roadworks,' Mitch assured him, perching on the edge of the desk. 'I came through them myself.'

'And arrived on time,' Richie pointed out sharply.

'Ah, well, be fair — my mother got me up and gave me breakfast,' Mitch said bravely.

'That'll be the little blonde this week, will it? Get off my desk!'

'If you've both quite finished?' Maggie asked coolly, her lips twitching. 'What did you want us for?'

'It's a special assignment,' Richie Lowell confided, his spectacles back on his nose, his mind back on business, 'and it's straight from above.'

'And what does God want?' Maggie sighed, knowing that if Mr Parnham, the owner, was interfering then this boded no good. She didn't like it already and she had no idea yet what it was.

'It's in Spain,' the editor said seriously. 'I'll just tell you a bit about it and then you can see.' Maggie didn't think she would see and her eyes met Mitch's sceptically. When Richie Lowell ignored late arriving, was prepared to discuss things reasonably and lowered his Australian voice to a coaxing murmur then suspicion loomed in her mind. She listened, however.

'The subject in question is Felipe de Santis, *Count* Felipe de Santis,' he said. 'He's thirty-six, extremely wealthy and two years ago he inherited the title. Until then, he was seen in every glossy place around the coasts of Europe, gambling, sailing his expensive yacht, entertaining the rich and famous and surrounded by beautiful women.'

'That sounds reasonable,' Maggie murmured sarcastically. 'About par for the course.'

'There's more,' Richie said hurriedly, determined to hold his audience. 'He dropped right out of sight then. No apparent reason, no warning. It happened almost overnight and for a long time nobody even heard of him.'

'Giant hangover?' Mitch offered, and got himself a glare.

'This is serious business!' Richie boomed, and Maggie quelled Mitch with a swift look.

'I'm getting interested,' she confided quietly. 'Go on.' She *was* interested because somehow or other the name rang a bell. Felipe de Santis? Why should she know the name? It was right at the back of her mind but she couldn't get it out.

'Now, it seems,' Richie went on, ignoring Mitch, 'that he withdrew to his place in Andalucía. Apparently he has a great estate beyond the Sierra Nevada — big hacienda or some such thing. He breeds horses and seems to be quite content to do that.'

'So?' Maggie asked. 'Why not? He's had a change of heart. Good for him. I'm not spying on him, so forget that if you've got any such idea.'

'It's not a question of spying,' Richie said urgently. 'He's agreed to let *Query* do an article about this place. It's an honour. Visitors are strictly discouraged normally.' He took a deep breath and looked fixedly at Maggie whose grey eyes were getting bigger and more icy with every word he said. 'You're to go to Spain to write an article about the countryside, the wildlife, this fabulous hacienda and the carefully bred horses. Mitch goes with you and takes the ncessary shots,' he added firmly, glancing at Mitch.

'You've got to be joking!' Maggie exploded with furious disbelief. 'My stories are serious, often political and of national interest. I'm not in the business of writing travelogues. In any case,' she added hotly before

Richie could open his mouth, '*Query* is a hard-hitting magazine, not some woman's paper!'

'I'm not joking, Maggie,' Richie said, looking a bit shamefaced at this straight-from-the-shoulder challenge. 'These orders came from the top, as I told you. Old Parnham knows the count from past times and had dinner with him a couple of days ago. This article about the hacienda was thought up then and when your name was mentioned Santis agreed. It appears that it's not because of your wonderful reputation, it's because you're a woman.'

'Indeed?' Maggie said stiffly. 'Bored at the old home-stead, is he? Forget it!'

'You'll not be alone with him, Maggie, he's got a sister, and in any case Mitch will be there,' Richie muttered, red with embarrassment. 'I told you it's from the top. It's not just that Mr Parnham knows the count, it's an idea the old boy's been floating for a while, so he tells me. He thinks we ought to have the softer article in from time to time.'

'Why pick on me?' Maggie asked fiercely. 'I'm not *soft*!'

'It will make a wonderful change,' Richie wheedled. 'It will show a different side to your writing. You'll be able to get all those glittering adjectives around the beautiful horses instead of your usual stuff. Mitch should get some magnificent shots.'

Mitch looked worriedly at Maggie. Her 'usual stuff' had built them both a fabulous reputation and in any case he wasn't too sure how she would take such a phrase. He was surprised to see her sitting almost dazed.

It was the words that had made her mind reach out and collect information from long ago. Beautiful horses, glittering, but, most of all, magnificent. She was momen-tarily back in time to when she was about thirteen, staying up to watch the glitter and excitement that the sight of one man had brought, watching every televised re-run as the whole country had gasped and applauded a young Spaniard whose handsome arrogance and amazing equestrian skills had held them enthralled.

Felipe de Santis! Felipe the Magnificent! It had to be the same man. He bred horses and the idea of a coincidence was too much to swallow. Why did he want an article on his hacienda? Maggie felt an odd excitement stirring inside.

In all probability, though, she wouldn't be allowed to do the article. He would be arrogant. He had looked haughty all those years ago. Then it had thrilled her. Now it would infuriate her. If he was a count he would be doubly arrogant and she would not be able to hold her tongue. The chances were slim indeed but now she really wanted to go. Her disciplined mind scoffed at the idea of such childish romanticism but some small stirring from the past brought this strange excitement that she should have outgrown and squashed with everything else.

'Right. When do we go?' She kept her thoughts well hidden and Richie looked mightily relieved, though a little suspicious.

'You meet him first—this evening at his hotel. You both go, although he doesn't know yet about Mitch—photography wasn't mentioned.'

'No photography on an article about wildlife and beautiful country?' Mitch enquired heatedly. 'What's he going to do? Offer the odd snapshot?'

'You'll go, you'll go,' Richie soothed. 'Go to meet him with Maggie and let her charm him.'

Mitch's eyebrows shot up. This was proving to be a memorable morning, Maggie accepting a 'soft' assignment and being volunteered as a charmer. She stood and turned to the door.

'OK,' she said quietly.

Behind her back, Mitch looked sceptically at his editor and Richie grinned, his gaze on Maggie's retreating figure. He rolled his eyes and blew her a kiss but unfortunately Maggie saw him do it.

'You should lose weight, Richie,' she murmured sweetly. 'It's all this sitting about you do.'

'And you should watch that tongue, Margaret Howard,' Richie rasped, glaring at her now that she had hit unerringly at his weak spot. 'Do you know what Margaret means? It means "like a pearl". You're more like a razor. You're going tonight to charm this count— Parnham's orders.'

Maggie just grinned and walked out and Richie glared at Mitch too.

'How did she get to be like that?' he asked irritably. 'Any woman likes a man to admire her.'

'Maggie does not admire men,' Mitch explained carefully. 'She was probably born like that.'

Maggie heard him and made a small rueful face. No, she hadn't been born like that. She had learned it the hard way and she never let her guard slip at all. She still bore the scars of battle, a battle she had nearly lost. Nobody had helped her in this wonderful, cultured city. She had been close to her own flat, the streetlights on, but she had fought alone. Now she needed no help at all. She had a hard shell like an oyster. It was the nearest she would get to being a pearl.

When Mitch met Maggie that night at the exclusive and expensive hotel where the count was staying he shook his head in despair. She did it deliberately, she really did. She was in trousers as usual, ignoring the fact that they might well be invited to dinner with the count. Her only concession to the occasion was that she wore silk, a green silk trouser-suit with the shirt open and a black camisole top beneath it. He was thankful she wasn't wearing boots but her hair had disappeared again under an awful black felt hat that looked as if it might have been her father's, and when she handed her coat in at the cloakroom she kept the hat on.

Even so, he admitted ruefully, she looked more alluring than any woman he knew, little blonde included, and there was that peculiar innocence that was so astonishing to anyone who knew her. He felt a stirring himself when he looked at Maggie although he certainly ought to have known better.

'Seen him yet?' Maggie came up, slinging her black bag over her shoulder, her shimmering grey eyes glancing around with interest. The bag just didn't go with silk: it was too big and bulky, no doubt stuffed full with notepads and pencils, Mitch observed, his photographer's eye altering her and becoming more exasperated with the hat every second.

'No. He's probably watching us from behind one of these pillars, making his mind up. You're going to antagonise him and get the idea scrapped, aren't you?' Mitch surmised, glancing down at her with a grin.

'As a matter of fact, no,' Maggie said seriously. 'You know me well, my friend. I did intend to do that at first. Describing the homes and environment of rich Spanish counts and their sisters is not my style. I'm more at home pursuing dictators and so are you. However, the more I thought about it, the more I imagined how nice it would be to have a really fabulous holiday in Andalucía. All free too.'

'Honestly?' Mitch asked with real surprise.

'Almost honestly.' Maggie grinned up at him. 'I might find something suspicious, you never know.'

Mitch smiled down at her; this was more like Maggie. She glanced at her watch impatiently. Was this the arrogance already—keeping them waiting as beings of little importance?

'Where the devil is that man?' she muttered. 'It's already seven-thirty.'

Mitch never had the chance to reply. A waiter came up and after one close look at them asked if they were waiting for Count Felipe de Santis. He had picked them out unerringly and Maggie assumed it was because they were clearly too poor-looking to be guests here. Mitch assumed it was because of Maggie's appalling hat. In

any case they were told that the count was waiting and
the waiter indicated the man who stood in the shadows
at the other side of the foyer.

Maggie saw him more clearly as he stepped forward.
The haughty face was older, harder, but it was the same
man she had dreamed of as a very young teenager. He
was not now in a tight black jacket, with silver trim-
mings on black trousers. There was no flat black Córdoba hat, but it was the same man and Maggie felt an
almost bitter rush of disappointment, so strong that it
took her by surprise.

Yes, it was the Felipe de Santis she remembered but
it was also the man she had had harsh words with this
morning—the driver of the red Porsche. She had not
recognised her hero because she had seen him as he
really was. Any lingering dreams died and she was
propelled back into her normal character speedily. She
was not now looking at him as a child looked. She saw
him clearly—arrogant as the devil and cold as ice, a
ready-made adversary.

He was dressed for dinner and she knew without
doubt that they were not going to be invited to join him.
Even the way he looked at them was enough to assure
her that they were way down on the social scale. Maggie
fastened her eyes on him and tried to get control of her
temper and her very stupidly lingering disappointment.

The count suddenly stiffened, his midnight-black eyes
narrowing to glittering points of light, and Maggie knew
the game was up. He recognised her too.

'Forget the trip,' she muttered to Mitch. 'I've met
him before. We almost came to blows. See how he's
looking at me?'

'He's probably shocked,' Mitch grated in a low voice.
'Take the bloody hat off: you're even scaring me.'

Maggie's temper and training didn't seem to be
helping at all at the moment. Those eyes seemed to be
holding her rigid. She was so mesmerised by their fixed
scrutiny that her action was purely mechanical. She

pulled the hat from her head and the shining mahogany hair flowed to her shoulders in a stream of dark red beauty that changed her appearance totally. There was still a little awe in her wide grey eyes and it added to the astonishingly innocent look that intrigued everyone.

For a second the count just stood there and then he came slowly across to them, his eyes never leaving Maggie's face until he was close. He stared at her intently, his gaze flashing over her long, gleaming hair, narrowing on her face and seeing the antagonism mixed with fascination. He was not at all affable and Maggie could not have expected it. For once in her life she was speechless. This man was a power. She was swaying between a long-lost dream and the rather alarming vision of reality. Right now she wondered how she had felt capable of raging at him this morning.

'Your Press card.' His hand came out imperiously and Maggie found herself fumbling in her bag like a thoroughly green reporter, anxiously trying to get it into his hand before he snapped his fingers, because she was sure inside that he would do that next.

She handed it over and his eyes scanned it rapidly.

'Margaret Howard,' he said coolly. He glanced at her derisively. 'In Spanish it is Margarita — so much better, so much more feminine, don't you think?'

A very unsubtle reminder of her aggression this morning and it brought Maggie back to life. She opened her mouth but Mitch took a tight grip on her arm and handed his own card across.

'Bruce Mitchell,' he stated firmly. 'Photographer. I work with Miss Howard.'

The count shot him a cold, hard look and then turned on his heel.

'I will conduct this interview in my suite; follow me,' he ordered, and Maggie began to boil quietly. The death of a hero and the birth of an enemy. She just knew it. He was too close for her to say a word to Mitch but she knew without doubt that he was going to turn on them as soon as the door to his suite was closed and say that he would not even consider having anyone like her in his home or even near it.

He surprised her.

'I have spent the afternoon reading your past features,' he informed Maggie icily, watching her now irritated face and ignoring Mitch completely. 'They were forwarded to me here at my request and I was impressed. You know your job; you even have a great talent.'

'Thank you,' Maggie managed to get out. She had not missed the fact that the coffee-table was piled high with past copies of *Query* and his arrogant manner was beginning to annoy her to such an extent that she was just about ready to storm off through the door and let Mr Parnham make of it what he could. Her momentary fascination was over. Here was a hero with icy eyes and a disdainful mouth — typically male! Only the thought of the pleasure she would have in telling him off when he told them they were not welcome in Spain kept her seated and in any way civilised.

'You may do the article,' he condescended, watching her intently and surprising her yet again. 'You have the ability to view things on a wide scale.' He glanced at Mitch and frowned. 'However, I cannot agree to Mr Mitchell's presence.'

'He's my photographer,' Maggie stated adamantly, before Mitch could get a word out. 'We work together.'

'You may bring a woman photographer,' Felipe de Santis said coldly, turning back to her with an astonished look that she should consider questioning him. He looked as if he was going to tell her to be quiet, and Maggie's temper rose.

'I work with Mr Mitchell or I refuse the assignment,' she snapped, her suspicions again aroused at this insistence on women only. She didn't know what he had in mind but Maggie fell for no tricks at all.

'Señor Parnham was very anxious to have the feature

written,' he said threateningly. 'He was also extremely careful to suggest you. I would remind you that he owns the magazine. Perhaps, Señorita Howard, you will refuse this assignment at the risk of your job?'

'Perhaps,' Maggie replied scathingly. 'It wouldn't matter much because I have a reputation, one that I'm really stretching to the full in doing a feature on sunny Spain. I don't do travel articles, *señor*. I'm not particularly interested in this and of course if I leave the magazine Mr Mitchell will leave with me. We're a team and he's the best photographer in the business. Any place will snap us up. I don't think we're under much threat.'

She looked at him with a derision of her own, delighted to be able to go into battle, and she was just standing to leave when there was a noise in another room of the suite as if something had fallen over. The count was on his feet at once, moving swiftly almost before the sound had stopped.

'*Momento!*' He motioned them both back to their seats and strode across to open a door but Maggie noticed that he also closed it behind him very firmly. Whatever was happening in there they were certainly not going to be a party to it. They heard a woman's voice but it was the deep voice of the count that carried to them most of all. He was soothing someone, his voice gentle, and when he came back into the room there was an altogether different look on his face. He looked worried, almost weary, and his eyes instantly found Maggie.

'I agree,' he said harshly. He looked at Mitch, studying him closely for the first time. 'If you are the best then obviously we want the best, especially as Señorita Howard will not move without you. Be warned, both of you, though, my hacienda is almost a kingdom. It is isolated, private and dangerous for intruders. You are coming to Andalucía to write about this place, to photograph it. You are coming for no other reason, understand that.'

'Could there be any other reason? We were given to understand that you asked for this article.' Maggie looked at him ironically and the dark eyes were turned fully on her, inspecting her face until she had the mad urge to shut her eyes and block out the intent gaze.

'I did not ask for it. I was persuaded. Before you leave Spain I will wish to read the feature. I will also wish to see every single photograph,' he warned in a hard voice. 'I made this arrangement with Señor Parnham. I value my privacy and I am prepared to defend it all costs. You will be in a position of trust, both of you. Do not betray that trust. I would make a very powerful enemy.'

'When do we come?' Maggie ignored the threats, her grey eyes steadily on him. There was no way a man was going to browbeat her and he had better know that right now.

'In two days. I return to Spain tomorrow. You will follow.'

'If it's so isolated then where do we stay?' Maggie enquired coldly, still meeting the dark, commanding eyes.

'You will stay with me, *señorita*,' he said softly. A slightly menacing smile edged his lips. 'The car will collect you at the airport and then you will be brought to the Hacienda de Nieve. From then on you will be exclusively in my territory.' The thought clearly gave him a lot of satisfaction but Maggie was not subdued.

'Good. It will be more convenient than travelling back and forth from some hotel. It will give me more chance to find things out. I can't write without information. You realise this, *señor*?'

'I realise it, Señorita Howard.' A flicker of admiration showed at the back of his dark eyes. He had alarmed her but she had stood up to him fearlessly and he knew it. It hadn't pleased him but he acknowledged it.

'*Adiós*, then. I will see you both in two days' time.'

Outside, Mitch let his breath out in a long sigh of relief.

'You'd better tell me how you met him and explain how we're going to stay there with him without bloodshed. You were both circling like gladiators. By the way,' he added, 'he had a woman in there with him.'

'I know.' Maggie looked at him thoughtfully. 'Did you hear what he said?'

'Perfectly,' Mitch assured her drily. 'I didn't understand it, though.'

'I did,' Maggie informed him. 'He said, "Stay here and I'll clear it all up later." He also said, "No, you cannot come out. I'll get rid of them." Now this may be a desire to get back to a sexy woman but the tone was all wrong. I think it was little sister.'

Mitch was thoughtful too for a moment and then he asked, 'Why didn't you tell him you spoke Spanish?'

'And hand over an advantage? No way! In any case, I'm not fluent. Let's just say I can find my way about in the language. It may be useful. Keep it secret.'

'No problem,' Mitch sighed. 'He'll never speak to me. You dislike men, Maggie. I think the count dislikes both sexes, or maybe it's just us?'

More than likely, Maggie mused. A man like that didn't have to threaten to be an enemy, he was ready-made for it, especially with her. How ironic that someone who had held her spellbound as a child and had lingered in her imagination for years should have turned out to be so arrogantly cold and superior. Still, she thought ruefully, most heroes would have feet of clay if studied closely.

# CHAPTER TWO

THAT night Maggie had a dream she had not had for over two years and woke up sweating and anxious, her own cries still ringing in her mind. Help me! Help me! She could see the iron railings of the park, the glitter of wet pavement. She was fighting and then beaten, the pain and the blackness as vivid in her nightmare as it had been in reality. She got up and made a cup of tea, sitting by her bed to drink it, her face pale and set.

Meeting Felipe de Santis had made her dream again. It was his coldness, his powerful masculinity. He was a man impossible to despise. One could only fear him or fight him, and she had chosen to fight long ago. The unspoken aggression of this evening had brought back the nightmare because with him she had gone further than mere temper. She couldn't just write him off. He had had too big an impact on her. It was a long time since she had been awakened by the dream — not since she had worked as a journalist with *Query* — but meeting Felipe de Santis had stirred it all up.

She lifted the hem of her nightie and looked determinedly at the scar on her thigh. She faced it from time to time, charged up her hate battery, reminded herself.

Would Felipe de Santis strike a woman, beat her, injure her? No. He would not; no instinct came to tell her he would. He was simply power, arrogance and power. He was not violence at all.

Had it been a woman in there, a woman staying with him, sleeping with him? Or had it been his sister? Why had he refused to let them meet her when they would certainly see her at the hacienda? There was something suspicious there. She would find out.

Maggie went back to bed but was a long time awake.

The hot panic of her nightmare faded and she thought about Spain. She had told no one at all but it had been the great dream of her life to go to Spain, the real Spain. Such dreams would not have fitted with her image and for years she had squashed them firmly, but they were still there and the name Andalucía had brought them racing back.

A dark, handsome face stayed in her mind, the present man mixed with the past dream. As a child she had feverishly researched everything she could about Andalucía because he came from there, the most southerly region in Spain, the most fascinating and the biggest, the land of guitars and castanets, the land of the swirling dresses and sharply stamping feet of flamenco dancers. She had searched for pictures and added them to her dreams, gypsies dancing, donkeys plodding through narrow streets, dazzling white houses and cool patios drenched in flowers.

It had never been possible to go, even though she had taken Spanish as an extra at university. She had clung to the hope even for that length of time, but it had never happened. Life had caught up with her, her job, her problems, but always at the very back of her mind the dream remained — Andalucía and a brilliant, handsome man on horseback, secret gardens with wrought-iron gates, fierce fighting bulls and beautiful Arab horses. The man was woven into her dream and even seeing him as he was had not exactly wiped the romantic image from her mind.

How idiotic! He was after all like every other member of his sex — merely a man with a man's desire to dominate. There would be trouble. She was quite sure of that. The wonderful world of dreams had better go. She would need all her wits about her.

Maggie was called to see Mr Parnham during the next morning and it came as a great surprise. The owner of the magazine was not normally available for comment if the Press at large wanted to interview him. He did not see lowly menbers of his establishment either and as Maggie got ready to go there were plenty of eyes watching her progress.

'It's got to be about this Spanish thing,' Mitch said quietly. 'He's going to tell you to go easy on his old buddy.'

Somehow, Maggie didn't think so. She had had plenty of time to mull things over and she was not too sure if there wasn't some underlying reason for this trip to Spain that they had not been told about, or maybe Richie didn't know himself. *Query* had been built on hard fact and delivered hard-hitting articles. She couldn't swallow this 'soft' line. Parnham was reputed to be as hard as his magazine. He had built it, guided it. Soft would not fit into his vocabulary.

She had to admit that he looked as hard as his reputation. Maggie was shown into a very expensive flat that overlooked the river and she had one of her rare glimpses of the owner as he stood with his back to a roaring fire and regarded her through eyes that were just as sharp as they had ever been in his youth.

Devlin Parnham was in his seventies but apart from the sparsity of his frame and a slight tendency to stoop you would never have known it.

'Miss Howard.' She was fixed with steely eyes and was somewhat surprised to find a decided twinkle there. 'They call you Maggie, don't they?'

'Er—yes.' Faced with the legend, she didn't know quite what to say. He didn't come quite under the heading of despised male sex but she was sure he had done at one time. Now, though, his age gave him untold advantages.

'Sit down and take your hat off. Don't like women in hats.'

Too stunned to be furious, Maggie sat and after a few seconds of close and silent scrutiny Devlin Parnham sat too, facing her across a magnificent Persian rug, with the fire banked as high as if it were mid-winter.

'I hear from Richie that you've agreed to go to Spain,' he remarked, looking at her closely. 'He's worried about that. He says you're tough and he's suspicious about this easy capitulation.'

Maggie found herself looking confused at this straight talking, and it appeared to delight the old man.

'I read everything you write,' he admitted. 'You're good, Miss Howard. That's why I want you in Andalucía. It might not be as soft as I've led Richie to believe.'

'I don't understand.' Maggie looked at him with interest and he nodded, seeing he had her complete attention.

'That's why you're here. I'm going to tell you.' He settled back and looked up at the ceiling as if he had forgotten she was there, and Maggie had the urge to creep away. He didn't look like the sort of man who let his mind wander, but you never knew after all. 'You might not remember Felipe de Santis,' he said suddenly. looking back at her keenly. 'Bit before your time.'

'I do remember him,' Maggie confessed ruefully. 'I was about thirteen. He was the great hero of everyone. I wasn't really one of those children who lived and breathed horses but he wasn't just a horseman, he was something very special—a once-in-a-lifetime sight.'

'Yes.' He nodded slowly. 'Very special. His mother was special too—meant a lot to me. I'm Felipe's godfather.'

'Are you?' Maggie didn't quite know what to say and he nodded again.

'I am. Not that I've had much chance to do anything for him. In the first place, he's wealthy and in the second place I never could get on with his father. Once Felipe's mother died I was not at all welcome. Icy cold man, the old count, and given to bursts of rage. Died two years ago of a heart attack.' He looked at Maggie quizzically. 'I'm old enough to be forgiven if I tell you that the news didn't sadden me. It meant that Felipe was in control of his own life with no battles.' He gave a great sigh. 'What he *has* got, however, is a problem, and that's where you come in.'

'I don't see what I can. . .'

'You're clever,' he pointed out. 'You're tenacious and you get at the truth. Truth is what I want. I have another godchild, Felipe's sister Ana. She's a sweet girl and she's not had much of a life for all their wealth. Ana is Felipe's problem because she's blind.'

'Oh. I'm sorry. Was — was she born blind?' Maggie was sorry. She couldn't think of anything worse and the old man looked gloomy.

'No. She's been blind since her father died. It happened suddenly and she's seen every specialist there is. *Nothing* is wrong with her sight. She's just blind for no reason. There must be a reason, though, and that's why I need you there, Miss Howard.' He looked at her fiercely. 'You're smart as two brass buttons. Go and find out, girl!'

'Does — does Mr — er — Señor de Santis want me to go out there?' Maggie asked worriedly, remembering the scathing remarks of last night.

'He doesn't. *I* want you to go! Felipe's dead against it. I pulled godfather rank and played on his guilt.'

'Why should he have guilt?' Maggie asked suspiciously.

'Because he wasn't there, girl! He wasn't there! He was in Málaga and when he came back his father was dead and his sister was blind. He has no reason for guilt but he feels it. That's why he agreed to this article on the hacienda.'

'So he knows why I'm going?'

'Er — vaguely.' He smiled at her a little evilly. 'I only have so much godfather rank. He wouldn't take kindly to an outsider coming to interfere and poke about. He's an Andaluz and they're proud. He thinks you're just writing an article. I told him we were softening up a bit. The rest is up to you.'

Thank you very much, Maggie thought bleakly,

eyeing him with even greater suspicion. He was sending her to face a hostile male and when everything was clearly laid down she was to spy on him — a thing she had refused so loudly.

'Suppose he finds out?'

'Charm him, girl! That's what women do best, isn't it?'

Maggie held her temper closely in check by sheer will-power. Who said his age excused him from being a male chauvinist? If she sprang up and gave him a good shaking, every bit of public sympathy would be on his side. She smiled rather grimly and said farewell. Out of the frying-pan, into the fire. Now all she had to do was fool Felipe de Santis and go against all her principles.

She knew she should refuse this assignment and even resign if necessary but to her annoyance she could still see the magnificent figure on horseback, she could still hear the music and the wild applause. She wanted to see the mantillas, the fans, the lace and pottery. She wanted to go there at last and peep through wrought-iron gates into beautiful gardens.

Most of all, though, she wanted to see this hacienda, this secret place lost in the mountains, and there was a mystery to solve. She squashed her conscience and kept the secret to herself. Mitch was not terribly subtle. He would give the game away within the first hour and Felipe de Santis would throw them out.

When they landed at Málaga it was hot, in spite of the fact that it was only the end of April. It was crowded too with holiday-makers on package tours, all eager to fling themselves on the nearest beach and sweat their way into a tan.

'I hope that man remembered to send his car,' Maggie muttered, looking around impatiently. 'I can do without this sort of thing.'

'There's a great holiday atmosphere,' Mitch pro-

tested. 'I could just sink into the crowd and go
unnoticed.'

'Except for the size of the camera over your shoulder,'
Maggie pointed out wryly. 'Anyway, give me the wide-
open spaces every time.'

'You should have been a big game hunter, Maggie.'

'I am usually,' she said softly. 'We've hunted plenty
of people, Mitch, and I've got the feeling that the count
is as dangerous in his own way. He's the kind of big
game that hunts you back if you put a foot wrong. Go
easy.'

'I'll be right behind you, boss.' He grinned down at
her, thankful there was no hat in sight. Even so, she had
tied her hair back and simply slammed it on top of her
head, If it hadn't been for the few feminine wisps that
escaped to frame that beautiful face she would have
looked forbidding.

The mouth was set grimly, he noticed, and the
trousers were there as usual, white jeans now with a
blue and white striped top, but there was the inevitable
shirt hanging open over it, as if she was ashamed of
anyone seeing those high, shapely breasts.

One day, he would get to the bottom of Maggie's
behaviour, although he knew he might have to get her
drunk first and she was even wary of sipping wine. No,
Maggie protected herself at all times. She was a total
mystery to him in spite of their long and successful
association. He always felt honoured to have been
chosen, because if she hadn't been comfortable with him
she would have worked him out of the job long ago with
little finesse. He kept his underlying masculine urges in
tight control with Maggie.

'Here we are, I think.' Maggie gave him a nudge as a
rather flustered man pushed his way to the front of the
people waiting and held up a placard — 'Señorita
Howard'. His eyes seemed to fasten on her immediately
and Maggie had the irritated feeling that he had been
given a very uncomplimentary description of her. Why

that should irritate her she did not know. She didn't care at all what Felipe de Santis thought about her. Having spoken to Devlin Parnham, she now understood the count's attitude at the hotel a little better. He had been persuaded to have them there and it didn't please him to have journalists foisted off on him. How he would take to having somebody prying she dared not think.

'I am Jorge, *señorita*,' the man said breathlessly, struggling with his English. 'I am to take you to the count. It will not take long — ten minutes, no more, depending on the traffic.'

Maggie and Mitch exchanged mystified looks as the man grabbed their trolley and began to wheel their luggage away vigorously.

'Ten minutes?' Maggie murmured. 'He's supposed to live in the land behind the mountains, isolated and lordly. What is he up to?'

'Maybe he's back to his old habits?' Mitch suggested. 'Or more likely he's at some hotel, waiting to search our luggage before we can proceed.' Well, she wouldn't be too surprised at that, Maggie mused.

'You're the chauffeur, then?' Mitch pried, helping to stow their luggage in the boot of a very large Mercedes.

'I am many things, *señor*.' Jorge grinned up at Mitch with some relief. Maggie had said nothing and he eyed her warily as if he had been warned to watch his step. 'All the servants at the hacienda have been with the count for years, some since he was a child.'

Maggie noted he did not say since *they* were children. This sister seemed to be carefully excluded from any conversation. In the hotel the count had merely said that they would stay with him, not with his sister and himself.

'Is the count's sister at the hacienda?' she asked offhandedly, trying to look bored. The man stiffened at once and shot a very keen look at her.

'*Sí, señorita*. I expect you will be allowed to meet her. Señorita Ana is always there.' He suddenly looked thoroughly miserable and Maggie let the matter drop. They would certainly meet her. It would be a bit tricky for the count to keep her shut away if they were staying with him.

It took just over ten minutes because the traffic was bad and they had to get clear of the airport. Not that the journey was far—they could almost have walked to the small airstrip, which was securely guarded. The Mercedes turned towards the runway and headed straight for a trim white and red plane that stood waiting.

'Well, this is how the rich live after all,' Mitch said quietly. 'I can't say that I mind. I wasn't particularly looking forward to a drive over mountain roads.'

Maggie wasn't too sure. It somehow seemed to be a cutting-off point, as if they were about to be flown away from any contact with civilisation. Once on board that plane they would be strictly at the mercy of the count. She felt as if he was closing a door behind them and right at this moment she would have liked to keep it open, if only just a crack, because Felipe de Santis walked round the plane and stood watching them as they came towards him.

He looked even taller. Broad-shouldered and lean-hipped, he still had that fluent, athletic look about him that had marked him out so long ago. In the Spanish sunlight his skin looked darker, more deeply tanned, and she would not have had to be told about his title. At the moment, *el conde* looked unspeakably arrogant.

He was more casually dressed than he had been in London. He wore dark jeans and a very expensive-looking soft T-shirt in pale blue, but he looked no more forgiving a person. The aura of power was there at once, tangible and quite alarming. Maggie's heart gave an uncomfortable little thump as those dark eyes were turned on them—no, on *her*! Once again he was ignoring Mitch and she felt he could read her mind. She was going to have to be very careful with this man or things would be bad.

'You had a good flight?' The burning black eyes skimmed over her and one dark brow rose ironically as he noted her trousers and the masculine shirt with rolled-up sleeves, the glorious hair piled ruthlessly on top of her head.

'Yes, thank you. It seems we're to face another flight?' Maggie looked straight back at him, making no attempt to smile; after all, he hadn't. He was like somebody carved from rock, handsome, hard and dangerous. He turned away with just a touch of impatience.

'The journey to the hacienda is difficult by car and quite a long way. I do not have the time to spare to meander through mountains. I do not like to be away for so long.' He raised his arm and a man came from the buildings at the side of the field, and it was soon apparent that he was taking the car away. Jorge was going with them.

'Do you keep the car here?' Mitch asked, venturing a question, having become tired of being treated as if he were invisible.

'It is rarely used—nowadays,' Felipe de Santis said shortly.

It told Maggie a lot, that and the look on his face. He came here now when he was obliged to come, and that would be rarely. He didn't like to be away from the hacienda for long. He had a blind sister to take care of. She felt a burst of sympathy but she firmly crushed it. That attitude would not help and it would not be welcome either. He looked as icily cold as he had done on the other two occasions she had met him.

She shot a secret look at him but he was checking the machine, the slight conversation with Mitch dismissed from his mind—or maybe not. There was an even tighter look on his face now, and when he pronounced that they were ready to leave Maggie was extremely thankful. It wasn't much fun standing beside a volcano.

Unfortunately she was sitting next to him—he was silently adamant about that. Apparently he thought that she and Mitch would get into no end of mischief if they were allowed to sit together in the back. Jorge was urged in beside Mitch and Maggie was firmly placed beside the count. He gripped her arm and pointed imperiously to the seat and she was glad to hurry and escape from his hard hand.

There was authority in that hand, authority she refused to recognise, and also the shock when he touched her was quite unexpected. She wished she had left her sleeves rolled down. Her skin was tingling and for some reason or other her face felt flushed. He had to admit he had a strange effect on her. Normally she looked down her nose at men and then ignored them unless they needed the sharp edge of her tongue. Something about Felipe de Santis made her slightly anxious and she held herself tightly in control.

Nobody attempted to speak until they were airborne and Málaga was left behind, and then to Maggie's surprise the count turned his head slightly, raised his voice and spoke to Mitch.

'You like aerial shots? Very soon the scenery will become most dramatic. I can get you to the necessary height if you have the lens for it.'

'Great!' Mitch recovered from surprise and dived into the leather shoulder-bag that contained his lenses. Felipe de Santis nodded and gave his attention back to the flight.

'You are always prepared?' he enquired with a certain amount of interest, leaning slightly back to address Mitch again.

'Naturally. It's what I do for a living. I may be able to get a good lead-in shot before we even arrive at the hacienda. As you said in London, Maggie works on a wide scope. I expect she'll want to see plenty.'

Felipe de Santis shot a dark, ironic glance at Maggie that quite caught her off guard. She had been watching him intently, looking for any sign that he was sceptical about this mission. He was. She had the decided feeling that he was on to her, and she hadn't even started yet.

'Maggie?' he murmured, his dark brows raised enquiringly.

'It's short for Margaret. I prefer it.' It was all she was prepared to say on the subject and he nodded as if he quite expected that.

'I prefer Margarita, but then you are not a Spaniard. You are a tough English lady, *es verdad?*'

Yes, it was true, Maggie thought tightly. She was tough and she was going to have to be. His attitude showed her that quite clearly. He was subtly changed now that they were flying to his mountain abode. She had threatened to refuse this assignment if Mitch was not allowed here, and Felipe de Santis had accepted that. Threats would now be of little use, and she knew it. She wondered why he had accepted it at all. It would have been a good excuse to use to get Mr Parnham off his back.

She had to admit that he worried her a lot. He might just be one jump ahead of her as he had been when he stole her car space. After all, he knew Mr Parnham better than she did and he didn't look as if he could be fooled at all. When she glanced at him, the hard mouth had actually softened to a smile but he was smiling to himself, thinking his own private thoughts, and Maggie bit into her soft lip, doing some rapid thinking of her own. Just what had she let herself be talked into?

The scenery was certainly spectacular, the sierras all around them, mountains climbing higher all the time, civilisation left well behind. Occasionally there were small, isolated villages, looking like white blossom carelessly tossed on the vast landscape. The mountain peaks and ridges clawed at the sky and Maggie stopped thinking altogether. The majesty of it stunned her. On the high mountains there was still snow but the valleys looked hot and dry. Over everything a deep blue sky sent out incredibly clear light. Sunlight glittered on the snow at the peaks and on the tiny white houses below.

It was a very different world, nothing she had expected. The villages were remote and became more so with every mile they flew. There were swift and dramatic changes of scenery, from towering mountains to beautiful, peaceful valleys, wooded and secret, places that looked as if no man had ever discovered them. There were unexpected stretches of open plain and then more sheer mountain walls.

'That valley!' Mitch leaned forward and yelled into the count's ear and instantly the small plane banked and screamed downwards like a stone from a catapult. Maggie's stomach seemed to stay behind somewhere up above and her hands gripped the edge of the seat anxiously.

It was not until they levelled out that she thought again about the possibility of living to a ripe old age. This was wild mountain scenery, the sparsely covered valley floor overhung by vast ochre-coloured crags, and Maggie shuddered at the thought of being stranded here. She had never been to Spain before but she had imagined it. Her imagination had never painted pictures like this, though, and she stole another glance at the man who held the plane steadily on its course as Mitch took his shots.

Felipe de Santis was like the land — proud, indomitable and alien. He flashed a glittering glance at her as if he felt her eyes on him and his gaze ran slowly over her face.

'You were afraid then?' he asked as softly as the noise of the plane allowed.

'I'm never afraid,' Maggie assured him firmly but her face flushed and his eyes moved to her hands, still tightly grasping the edge of the seat. She relaxed them instantly but it was a little too late. He looked back at her, satisfaction in the dark, probing gaze.

'There is a woman in you after all,' he murmured. 'I really was beginning to wonder.'

Maggie refused to answer. She was not about to be drawn into any argument with the count and she was shakily aware that any of her usual remarks would bring swift retaliation, probably spectacular aerobatics that would have her screaming and confessing madly to the sin of femininity.

'Stop worrying,' he said quietly. '*Todo esta bien*. We will soon be there. The Hacienda de Nieve is just over the mountains.'

But which mountains? Maggie asked herself, looking round as the plane gained height and Mitch carefully put his camera away. As far as she could see there was nothing at all but mountains and she had a nasty feeling that they would be isolated behind them for some considerable time to come.

'Is it all mountains?' she asked rather worriedly. She knew perfectly well that it was not, but to her surprise nerrves were getting the better of her.

'You are speaking of Andalucía?' He glanced at her with a great deal of arrogance. 'There are thirty-four thousand square miles of Andalucía, *señorita*. It stretches from the endless beaches of the Costa del Sol and the Costa de la Luz, to the snowy peaks of the sierras and great plains where the fierce black bulls graze. Andalucía has everything, *is* everything. It has been called the flower of Spain.'

'Forgive me for not knowing,' Maggie murmured sarcastically, annoyed at this haughty lecture. 'I spend a lot of my time in jungles and war-torn cities.'

'I know. I have read your work,' he countered quietly. 'It leaves me wondering why you should have been chosen for this very tame assignment. Perhaps they are giving you a rest?'

'I really don't know,' Maggie lied swiftly.

'I am to believe that they dare to send you on an

assignment without discussing it with you, *señorita?* How brave they must be.'

He said nothing else and Maggie quite understood the subtle insult. She was a tough English lady who was not at all feminine and who would physically attack anyone who stood in her way. He wasn't fooled either. He had summed up his godfather and he had summed her up too. This was a sheer waste of time. He would probably land and then tell them to walk back. When she glanced at him again he looked very grim and she wondered if she should have told Mitch that he might well have a lot of opportunity to photograph Spain — on foot as he walked back to Málaga.

The hacienda came as a total surprise. One moment they seemed to be flying through and over mountains and the next they were skimming over a long, fertile valley, turning to come in with the wind and losing height steadily. It was not like some of the valleys they had seen so far, sparsely vegetated and arid. It was green, lush and luxuriant, ringed by the mountains with snowy peaks.

She could see waterfalls cascading down some of the mountain-sides and in the distance a lake. From the air she was able to see the whole length of the valley and she could only guess at its size. It was richly covered with trees, glinting in the sunlight, a land hidden in mountains, completely cut off. There were roads but they skirted the mountains and looked dangerous even from this height. There was no sign of the great plains the count had spoken of. It was an ideal place to hide away.

'My home,' Felipe de Santis said quietly and Maggie saw, at the head of the valley, the most fabulous place she had ever seen in her life. Even in these towering mountains, its majesty and grandeur impressed. Backed by the dark foothills, the hacienda stood proudly alone, slightly forbidding and clearly impregnable.

It was huge, red-roofed and white-walled, the main house on a slight rise inside the high-walled perimeter. The entrance through the surrounding wall stood high and splendid, arched in the Spanish manner, and the vast wrought-iron gates stood open, ready to close behind them and looking as if they would.

Maggie's heart lurched for many reasons. There would be no slipping away here, no going to ground to mull things over. She was tackling this man on his own terms and at some time she would be doing it head-on. Always before she had worked free, able to move about at will. Now she was about to enter a stronghold, because this was the count's world, his kingdom behind the mountains, and the grim satisfaction on his face told her he was well aware of it.

'It's superb!' Maggie felt the need to say something and, in any case, the words were almost torn from her. It gained the count's immediate attention and he looked sardonically surprised.

'You are making an unsolicited comment, Señorita Howard? You must be impressed. I will give you a quick tour from the air,' he added just as she opened her mouth to give him a caustic reply.

The plane rose, banked again and he circled the vast complex that was the Hacienda de Nieve. Around the main house were many smaller buildings, all white with the same red-tiled roofs that made the house so elegant. This mixture of sizes did nothing to detract from the overall beauty of the place; rather they gave interest, drawing the eye to different shapes and heights.

'Servants' quarters, stables, storehouses and so on,' Felipe de Santis pointed out.

'And that?' Maggie indicated a large building almost as big as the main house itself.

'That? It is where we train the horses.' He said nothing more and Maggie shot him an intrigued look. Was this where he had trained as a young man? Had the brilliance he had shown been nurtured here? She stared at his profile, trying to see in him her old hero, and he shot her an intrigued look as he felt her eyes on him. It had Maggie looking away quickly and she was glad to be able to say something.

'A swimming-pool!' As they flew over the house and looked down on colourful gardens she could see a pool of some considerable size, glittering greenly in the sun, tubs of geraniums around it. 'Where do you get your water, so far away from civilisation?'

It somewhat restored his sardonic humour.

'We are isolated but quite civilised,' he remarked drily. 'Water is from many wells, pumped up and sterilised on the property. Not that it would harm us to drink it as it comes. The snow from the mountains keeps the supply constant. It is also icily cold. We use solar heating for the pool.'

And I've no swimsuit! Maggie fretted silently. There was something so grand about this place that she felt momentarily detached from her usual character. She hadn't bought a swimsuit for years.

The horses that the count reared were also in evidence, some actually in the railed compounds dotted around the place, and beyond, towards the mountains, Maggie could see well-fenced fields with white and grey horses roaming peacefully. At some time or other he would have to go out to these. It would give her time to explore and investigate and she would have to pick her time carefully because she had the feeling that Felipe de Santis would be keeping them well in his sight and strictly under his thumb. He might have been persuaded to have them out here but he would not let them be any sort of nuisance, and she was well aware of it.

There was a great deal of activity as they landed. The small airstrip was well away from the house and even before they turned to land a car had left the property and was heading out to meet them. Maggie looked down and saw it moving at some speed; dust flung up in a stream behind it and it was waiting as they taxied to a halt.

The count simply abandoned the small, expensive aircraft and led them to the car. No doubt there were minions in plenty to see to the plane and Maggie noted that his sister had not come rushing to meet him in the car. Well, it would not be long before things became clear. She was actually in the combat zone now and she noted uneasily that once again she was placed firmly beside the count.

# CHAPTER THREE

THE house was built on a rectangle that surrounded an inner courtyard and Maggie's steps dragged a little as they walked into this. The perfect condition of everything had somewhat disguised the extreme age of the place, but now it was obvious. Columned arcades that led to the house surrounded this inner court, and as she looked up Maggie saw that this arrangement was duplicated above, making an elegant balcony that overlooked the courtyard below. French windows opened from the bedrooms, and they were open now, white silken curtains swaying in the breeze.

There were flowers everywhere. Hanging baskets with bright geraniums decorated the higher balconies and the courtyard had been turned into a spectacular garden, tubs of potted plants adorning the old paving. It was hot in this enclosed space, the smell of plants and flowers intoxicating. A small fountain splashed musically in the centre, the clear water dazzling, and Maggie found herself almost stunned for the first time in many years.

'Why didn't you have the pool in this hot little spot?' she enquired almost thoughtlessly.

'And ruin architectural magnificence?' Felipe de Santis asked scathingly. 'It is a question that takes me utterly by surprise as you obviously admire all this. Perhaps words are springing unbidden from your lips, *señorita*? This is not the first time you have ventured comments without the necessity to drag them from you.'

True, Maggie admitted silently, tightening her lips. She would have to watch it. She had no intention of charming him. In any case, even if she had been a

42

skilled charmer it was not possible to allure somebody who slashed back at you like a master swordsman and drove the point in. He would find anybody's weak spots and he didn't seem to have any himself.

'You have controlled the urge to speculate?' he enquired sardonically. '*Todo es normal?*'

Maggie had the greatest desire to answer in Spanish and confound him, but in the first place she wasn't exactly up to it, and secondly she was keeping it under her hat. It might give her an advantage at some time. He seemed to have a tendency to goad and that would quite clearly lead to trouble. She did not want trouble; she wanted action, information and a speedy departure. This was not her normal work and there was absolutely no room for manoeuvre.

Mitch was lingering behind, busily clicking away with his wonderful camera and Maggie stifled the need to remind him not to waste his film. Still, it was very beautiful and, after all, there was an article to write, they would want background shots. It was all good for the camouflage in any case, and she would need plenty of that with Felipe de Santis.

There was no anticlimax as they entered the house; it was grand, spacious and still very Spanish. From the large entrance hall, old oak doors and passages led off to other parts of the house, a large open staircase facing them. The count led them through one of the doors into what was a very beautiful drawing-room and almost immediately a servant came in with refreshments.

'Your luggage will be taken to your rooms,' Felipe de Santis said coolly, inviting them to sit. 'It would perhaps be as well to rest before dinner. Time enough to start your work tomorrow. You will be shown to your rooms when you are ready.'

He looked as if he might just be going to stride off and leave them and Maggie was quite relieved. She was getting to be very wary of those dark eyes and their constant probing. She wasn't quite sure what he was summing her up for but he was certainly doing that. However suspicious he was, he surely realised that he had agreed to this visit? She told herself firmly that he did not suspect a thing, but he suddenly slanted a brilliant glance across at her and she wasn't at all sure what he thought. He was secret, powerful and looked ruthless. When he looked at her like that she wasn't at all sure that this was in any way a 'soft' assignment.

Whatever his intentions had been, he did not get the chance to stride off. There was the sound of light footsteps in the hall and the door was suddenly thrown open as a young girl stood there and smiled brilliantly. She was utterly beautiful, large dark eyes in a small vivid face. Her hair was black as jet, falling beyond her shoulders, straight and heavy, blue lights glittering along its length. Her short, expensive dress showed a slender figure and the hands that were held out towards Felipe de Santis were as small and elegant as the hands of a dancer.

'You're back!' She spoke in Spanish, her head held at an angle of listening, and Maggie shot a quick look at their host. The forbiddingly handsome face was softened, his lips curved in a smile.

'*Sí*, I am back and not too long, eh? I have brought visitors with me. You must speak in English or they will not understand.'

The smile died slowly on the girl's face, her slender figure frozen. She took a slight step forward and then stopped, her face turned towards the count.

'Felipe?'

'It is quite all right, Ana,' he assured her softly. 'There is nothing in your path.' He never moved but waited for her to come to him, and when she did his arm came around her with a swift, protective action that was not lost at all on Maggie. She heard Mitch's swiftly indrawn breath and then Felipe looked across at them intently.

'My sister Ana,' he introduced quietly. The girl

turned her head, following the direction of his voice, and the smile was back on her face at once. She was safe with her brother and Maggie realised how great was his burden. Mitch looked stunned and she felt an incredible burst of guilt that she had not told him about this girl's problem.

Ana de Santis was about nineteen. The beautiful eyes seemed to have the same dark depths as those of her brother but they did not have his sharp, probing gaze. Their liquid depths were sightless. She was quite perfect and that those eyes could not see was a great tragedy, one that Maggie felt deeply at that moment.

She never waited to be asked; she came straight forward and spoke.

'Hello. I'm Maggie Howard.' She took the small, graceful hand and squeezed it firmly. 'I'm a journalist.'

'Maggie?' Ana de Santis looked puzzled, her head tilted questioningly, and Maggie smiled to herself. This must run in the family.

'It's short for Margaret,' she said, adding wryly, 'In Spanish, it's Margarita.'

'Ah! I understand.' Ana smiled that lovely smile again and Felipe looked closely at Maggie, a slight smile edging his lips too.

'And this is Señor Mitchell,' he introduced as Mitch came up, his eyes riveted on the girl's face. 'He is a photographer who works with Señorita Howard.'

'Hello.' Mitch was very quiet. He seemed to be mulling things over because he must have seen that this had not been the shock to Maggie that it had to him.

'Señor Mitchell.' She was all Spanish dignity with amazing rapidity, her face suddenly polite and much more grown-up. Now she did not look like a young girl, she looked like the sister of a count, and Maggie stepped into the breach swiftly.

'I'm writing about this beautiful place, *señorita*. I need a photographer and I work with Señor Mitchell. He's the very best. We won't be here long and we'll try not to get in your way.'

'Oh! I do not mind, Señorita Howard. I did not mean to make you feel unwelcome. Sometimes it is difficult to meet new people.'

'You didn't make us feel unwelcome,' Maggie said emphatically. 'I think we're both a bit stunned that you're so beautiful. And please call me Maggie.'

'Maggie,' the girl said experimentally. 'It is strange.'

Maggie felt strange too. It was like being in a minefield. One wrong step and Felipe de Santis would pounce.

'Señor Mitchell is normally called Mitch. His real name is Bruce but he never answers to it.' She cast an impatient look at Mitch, who was standing with the same stunned attitude he had adopted when he had seen that the girl was blind. He wasn't helping at all. 'He's harmless, quite afraid of me.'

It brought a very visible relaxing of attitudes that quite surprised Maggie. She didn't know she had it in her but she had felt the need to act. Ana de Santis was a charming girl and it was necessary to get close to her if she was to carry out her orders. It wouldn't help if the count exploded with rage. Obviously he had not warned his sister of this visit.

Maggie was sure now that this had been the girl in the hotel in London. She was equally sure that she had not known who was speaking to her brother too. He had dropped all this on her as a shock. If this was his way of helping her then Maggie didn't think much of it.

She shot a reprimanding look at the count and found that as usual he was watching her intently.

'Perhaps you would both like to see your rooms and sort out your possessions,' he murmured quietly and Maggie nodded impatiently. 'I will get someone to show you the way,' he added, reaching for the bell.

'I look forward to meeting you at dinner,' Ana said, the lovely, blank eyes turned to them. A shy and tentative smile came to the girl's face and then she turned and went out of the room, walking as surely and as gracefully as if she could see just like everyone else. Jorge came in then and stood at the door.

'Show Señor Mitchell to his room,' Felipe de Santis ordered and when Maggie too turned to the door he detained her. 'I would like a word with you, Señorita Howard, if you please,' he said firmly. 'Jorge will come back for you when he has settled Señor Mitchell.'

With no alternative, Maggie waited, and as the door closed he turned to her and regarded her coolly.

'Please sit down, Señorita Howard. I think this is a good time for confessions.'

When she sank to the seat she had recently vacated he paced about a little and then swung to face her, his dark eyes angry.

'You will now tell me about your mission,' he commanded harshly. 'And do not deny anything,' he added as she opened her mouth to speak. 'I know Devlin a little better than he imagines and I was not at all fooled about this easy assignment of yours.'

'Then why did you agree to it?' Maggie gave him a challenging look and he frowned impatiently.

'Do not fence around with me,' he snapped. 'I want to know exactly what you are doing here. I have no doubt that a brilliant article will appear but I am not at all fooled that someone of your peculiar talents would either be asked or would agree to such an easy exercise. You are therefore here because of Ana. In other words, *señorita*, Devlin Parnham has sent you. What are your orders?'

'I'm to discover why Ana is blind.' There was little point in denying anything and he stared hard at her, his lips in one straight, angry line.

'You have a very high opinion of yourself. Ana has seen every important specialist in Spain. My trip to London was on Ana's behalf, my last throw of the dice. She went to see a very eminent specialist, and to no avail. All I know is what I have known for the past two years: there is no reason at all for the blindness. She cannot see because she does not wish to see. It is perfectly genuine with Ana and not at all uncommon, as I am given to understand. You imagine that you can succeed when so many experts have failed? She has seen doctors, psychiatrists, everyone!'

'It wasn't my idea,' Maggie pointed out coldly. 'As you seem to have seen through the subterfuge from the very first moment, why did you agree to this trip?'

'Maybe I am clutching at straws, scraping the bottom of the barrel? I do not know what to do next. Perhaps I am prepared to wait for a miracle. I had every intention of refusing when I interviewed you but I had read your articles. You are certainly unlike any other woman I know.'

'There seemed to be some doubt in your mind about my exact gender,' Maggie put in drily, and he cast her an irritated look, his dark eyes running over her again as she sat facing him, her hands in the pockets of the loose shirt.

'You're a woman,' he growled. 'I have no doubt about that, otherwise you would not annoy me so frequently.' He stood abruptly and took to pacing about again. 'Maybe you can help. You have an analytical mind. You are purposeful, determined. You have a way of finding out truths and you are a woman. Ana may confide in you as she would never confide in me. I agreed to this trip because of that. I am prepared to try anything.'

'Don't tell Ana,' Maggie said urgently and he spun round to glare at her.

'Do I look like an idiot?' He didn't. He looked fiercely alarming and in actual fact she hadn't the faintest idea how to begin this task.

'I'll try my best,' Maggie said worriedly. 'It's all I can do.'

'It is all any of us can do,' he assured her sombrely. 'Does Señor Mitchell know about this hidden task?'

'Not as yet. I may have to tell him, though.'

'As you wish,' Felipe de Santis snapped. 'Whether he knows or not, however, keep him away from my sister.'

'What exactly do you mean by that?' Maggie enquired angrily, jumping to her feet. 'If you're implying. . .'

'I am not implying, *señorita*! I am issuing an order. I have little doubt as to why you insist on his presence. Just see to it that he does not also cast his eyes on Ana.'

'I would like to go to my room now, Señor de Santis.' Maggie looked at him heatedly then turned away, fuming steadily.

'You will help me?' He spoke without any sign of softening or apologising and Maggie's temper rose a little higher.

'Help you? Certainly not!' She turned back to glare at him. 'I'll help your sister willingly if I can, but never you. I have an article to write. If, while I'm doing that, I see the chance to help Ana then I will, for her sake, not yours. If no opportunity arises then I'll finish my task and go. I'm not a member of the medical profession.'

Jorge suddenly appeared at the door and Maggie did not wait to hear any answer; she walked out of the room, scooping up her bag and swinging it over her shoulder, quite satisfied that this time Felipe de Santis had come off worst.

In the quiet of the beautiful room overlooking the perfumed courtyard, Maggie summed it all up. Just what did she know now? Ana de Santis was blind with no reason but some deep psychological decision to be so. Her brother did not know the reason and needed a woman to get close to her, and he was prepared to put up with both Mitch and herself to get to the bottom of things.

Maggie walked out on to the balcony and looked

across at the mountains. She did not trust the count even though she admitted that he had a strange effect on her. There were many secrets flying about and he had some of his own. Just how secluded was his sister? The girl was obviously devoted to him and there was no fear there. Something had happened two years ago that had been traumatic enough to send Ana de Santis blind. Was it something to do with her father's death? This was going to be very tricky.

She began to unpack, trying to puzzle things out, and when a knock came on the door she opened it without thinking, her mind still elsewhere. The sight of Felipe de Santis brought her back to the present with a bang. He just stood there and looked at her and Maggie held his gaze for a moment before inviting him in. It was clear he had more to say and she might as well get it over with in one go.

'You wish to speak to me, *señor*? Come in.'

'Our conversation did not end to my satisfaction,' he informed her tightly, coming in and closing the door. 'I wish to impress on you that the rules I made in London still stand. You are here to write about the Hacienda de Nieve, the countryside around and the horses. That I need assistance does not mean that I will be more lenient or less vigilant.'

'Naturally,' Maggie agreed ironically. 'I never expected anything else. You want both the biscuit and the bun.'

'I do not understand you,' he rasped, 'but coming from you I imagine it is some acid comment. I will be watching both of you closely and I will want to see everything that is to be published.'

'*You* are wanting the favours!' Maggie reminded him angrily.

'And you have orders from Señor Parnham,' he pointed out silkily. 'I very much doubt if you would be willing to walk away now in any case. You have a reputation of not letting go of a thing once you have started and you would be delighted to discover that I am responsible for Ana's blindness. I understand you, *señorita*.'

'I doubt it.' She turned away impatiently and opened another case. If he didn't go soon she would explode. She couldn't just ignore him in his own house and she had the nasty feeling that she would not have been able to ignore him anywhere. And he was right in one way — she would love to get the better of him very decisively.

'Why do you do that with your hair?' He suddenly snapped the question at her, taking her by surprise.

'None of your business!' Maggie spun round and glared at him wide-eyed. 'If you understand me so well you'll know what I think of a man's opinions.'

He stood and looked at her for a moment longer, his eyes running over her scathingly, taking in the beautiful, angry face, the wide and annoyed grey eyes and the tall, slender figure concealed in such efficient garments. He strode to the door and then slanted a look at her that was all sardonic speculation.

'You have a problem of your own, *señorita*,' he murmured ironically. 'Perhaps before you help my sister you should help yourself.'

Maggie was left staring at a closed door, lost for words. Just who did he think he was? She ran his crimes rapidly through her mind. He wanted help but he wouldn't give an inch about anything. He didn't trust her one bit either and he thought she was having an affair with Mitch. He had the cheek to make personal remarks and expect no retaliation whatever. Oh, it was going to be absolutely wonderful here. She might just waylay him and hit him with something heavy!

He had great advantages too. Obviously Devlin Parnham had been prepared to agree to any sort of conditions to get the count to accept this mission. It gave Felipe de Santis all the cards. He could order her about and lay down any rule he thought of.

Dinner would be an ordeal. Maggie was filled with resentment about the count and chose her most severe outfit just to show him what she thought of his beliefs. She wore a black silk trouser-suit, the jacket reaching her hips and hanging loose. It buttoned almost to the neck, just showing a white lace top.

She spent a lot of time on her hair, making quite sure it was fixed on top of her head with not one softening wisp showing, and apart from a little eyeshadow and a small amount of pale lip-gloss she dispensed with the make-up. Looking at herself in the mirror, she was very satisfied. She looked daunting and she went downstairs all geared up for trouble. What did he mean — a problem? She had dealt with her problems years ago.

They were already in the *sala*, having a pre-dinner drink, when Maggie walked in, and she knew that at least one pair of dark eyes watched her sardonically. The girl looked lovely, Maggie decided. She wore a pale pink dress that swirled around slender legs and her hair was caught back with a matching headband. It was Ana who came forward as Maggie came into the room, and clearly she did not let her blindness get in the way of being hostess for her brother.

'Señorita Howard? Can we get you a drink?'

Maggie was about to refuse but she caught that sceptical look in the count's eye and changed her mind.

'Thank you. A dry sherry, please.'

'Is that a compliment to Spain or a safe bet, Señorita Howard?' the count asked tauntingly. 'Sherry is one hundred per cent Spanish. Even the name is an English mispronunciation of Jerez.'

'I think it was a safe bet, *señor*,' Maggie said stiffly. 'I don't drink.'

'A precaution?' he enquired sardonically. 'I sincerely hope you will take wine with the meal, *señorita*. Should you decide to stick to sherry and branch out into the heavier aloroso you will have a thick head tomorrow and we will have an entertaining evening.'

Maggie had a tremendous urge to simply say, Shut up! but she curbed her impulse and managed a rather sour smile, very grateful when Ana came across to her.

'You look wonderful,' she said quietly and Ana's face flushed with pleasure.

'Do I? Do I really? The trouble with being blind is that you cannot see yourself. I have a servant who helps me but always I wonder if she is telling me the truth or merely being kind.'

'She's telling the truth,' Maggie assured her. 'Pink suits your dark colouring. You couldn't look better.'

At this point the count came up with Maggie's drink and conversation lapsed, but Maggie felt it was a start. This girl did need a woman around her and her brother's face was a fascinating mixture of satisfaction and irritation. Maggie had not one doubt about who irritated him.

Dinner was delightful. There was a delicious ice-cold soup with *tostones*, croutons, chopped pimiento and chopped cucumber, which were added as it was served. 'It is *gazpacho andaluz*,' Ana told her when she murmured how much she was enjoying it. 'It is eaten in many other parts of Spain now because it is so good.'

For the main course there was *pato con peras*, duck with pears, and, later, fresh fruit and a caramel cream *flan*. Maggie sipped cautiously at the wine, aware all the time of dark, sardonic eyes watching her.

It was a hard time. Maggie had to work at things because Mitch was very different from his usual amusing self. He was brooding and she hadn't the faintest doubt about why. She would have to confess later.

In the end, Maggie's patience quite evaporated.

'How do you pass your time here?' she asked Ana outright. 'How do you fill your days? Don't you miss the city life?'

Felipe looked thunderous, his sardonic amusement going swiftly, but Ana took it well after a brief little pause.

'I swim, ride and I am learning Braille. I manage to fill my days quite well.'

'Isn't it dangerous for you to swim and ride?' Mitch asked quickly, forgetting his silence for a moment, and to Maggie's relief the lovely young face was turned to him, Ana smiling.

'Not at all. I know the pool. I know how long it is, how deep, and one does not forget how to swim. I do not need to see. I ride only with Felipe or when he is near. I have a special horse. You will photograph our horses, Señor Mitchell?'

'Oh, I intend to.' Mitch began to talk normally and Maggie willed him not to ask Ana to show him these horses her brother reared. It would have filled the count's dark face with fury and suspicion. Mitch said nothing about it and Maggie relaxed.

She noted though that after this Felipe de Santis was prepared to acknowledge Mitch's presence although he was stiffly formal. She was able to chat to Ana for most of the meal and what with one thing and another she felt some progress had been made, though what she was doing in this situation she did not know.

It was a long way from the back streets of big cities and the criminal set, and even further from the grim-faced soldiers who had guarded her last assignment. She wasn't too sure how long she could keep this up. Only Ana's predicament made it possible — that and a sneaky feeling of how wonderful it would be to get the better of *el conde*.

After the meal she escaped as soon as she could and found herself walking up the stairs with Mitch. He was very quiet and she decided to tell him there and then.

'Come in here a bit,' she suggested as they came to her room, 'I'd better tell you a secret.'

Mitch needed no second bidding and Maggie shut the door firmly behind them, getting on with her confession at once.

'The count actually asked you to help too?' Mitch

asked after she had told him about Devlin Parnham's orders. 'How can you?'

'She has no real cause for blindness,' Maggie told him. She flung herself on the end of the bed and began to bring him further up to date.

'Apparently she's seen plenty of specialists and they all say the same thing—she's blind because she refuses to see.'

'Is it possible?'

'Yes. I've heard of it before. Sometimes people can't speak for the same sort of reasons, but it's always got to be something traumatic that's happened. The count *says* he doesn't know what happened.'

'And you don't believe him?'

'Not really.' Maggie shook her head and looked thoughtful. 'He asked me to get close to her and try to find out. He thinks a woman might be able to do it.'

'She's awfully sweet and natural, don't you think?'

'Yes.' Maggie shot a look at him. 'Don't go too close to her, chum. Big brother will be keeping an eye on things.'

'I've no intention of going near her,' Mitch assured her indignantly. 'She's nothing more than a teenager!'

'She's about nineteen.'

'Didn't I just say so?' He shot a very cross look at Maggie but gave in almost at once. 'All that aside, though, this should give us a lot more loose rein here.'

'No way! Never believe that,' Maggie informed him wryly. 'The same rules apply as stated in London. No snooping, no prying, show him everything. Old Parnham agreed to that.'

'And yet he wants your help?'

'The count is a man who only follows his own rules. He's not much concerned with other people's feelings or wishes. I suppose I can be grateful that he didn't actually order me to help,' she finished drily. 'Though, on consideration, I'm not sure he didn't.'

'Oh, well. Tomorrow we'll start the assignment,' Mitch said, standing to leave. 'You'll have to slot your Aunty Maggie bit in when you can. By the way,' he added, standing at the now open door, 'you looked very sexy tonight.'

'*What*?' Maggie shot to her feet and stared at him in astonishment, and at that moment Felipe de Santis walked past the room, his dark eyes taking everything at one swift glance — Mitch obviously just leaving, Maggie's suddenly flushed face and wide eyes and the slightly rumpled bed where she had rested to talk to Mitch. What he thought was clear, and Maggie's cheeks flushed even more. It was sheer outrage but to him it must have looked like guilt. He made no comment and, having got away with his last remark, Mitch left too.

Maggie stared at herself in the mirror. Sexy? She looked as efficient as a hospital matron, as cool as a cucumber. She got ready for bed and never looked at herself again but it was hard to bring her mind back to Ana's problems and the great mystery of the hacienda. She kept seeing dark, intent eyes, scornful eyes in a starkly handsome face.

Over the next few days Maggie slowly got closer to Ana de Santis. It was not too difficult. The girl clearly missed having a woman around who was closer to her age than the rather stiff-faced servants who ran the great hacienda. There was every comfort and luxury and Maggie became quite attached to her lovely room. She was free to wander all over the estate and Mitch kept with her, his collection of shots growing.

So far they had not ventured beyond the great boundary walls; many times Ana came with them and this was allowed after Felipe noticed Maggie's protective attitude to the girl and the gentle way that Mitch dealt with her. All the same he watched them like a cold-eyed hawk, and Maggie knew they must not put one foot wrong, favour or not.

Ana seemed to be almost hungry for company and she took to coming along to Maggie's room to chat, although she never spoke of her blindness and Maggie ventured no questions. It was much too early for that.

'What does Señor Mitchell look like?' Ana asked one afternoon as she sat with Maggie in the cool of the upstairs balcony.

'He's very fair,' Maggie told her. 'He has blue eyes, quite bright blue. He's good-looking and he's tall, though not as tall as your brother.'

'He is nice, Maggie?'

'Well, I think so. I've worked with him for nearly two years. Sometimes we've been in danger. He's always reliable. He tries to protect me even when I don't need it.'

'Why do you not need protection?' Ana asked, and Maggie smiled to herself.

'I'm tough. Do you want to know what I look like?'

The answer shook Maggie to the core.

'Oh, no. I already know how you look. Felipe told me. I wish I could see you for myself all the same.'

'You're not missing much,' Maggie said wryly, quite sure that Felipe de Santis would have already acquainted his sister with this fact.

'That is not what Felipe says. He says you are extremely beautiful. He says you have hair like dark sunlight with flecks of gold as if the sun is trying to get through. Your skin is like creamy blossom and your eyes are so clear and grey they can see into the soul. He told me all that very carefully.'

Maggie's face flushed hotly and she was glad that Ana could not see her at that moment.

'He's being kind to you — protecting you from the truth.'

'Oh, no! He was very thorough, very detailed. He always helps me to see. He also said that you attack like a well-trained guard dog. He says you give no quarter.

According to Felipe you would be a good man to have on his side in a fight.'

Would she really! There was little chance of being on his side at all as far as Maggie was concerned. It took a great deal of acting skill not to show her vast irritation. She was still quietly fuming at dinnertime and Mitch looked at her warily, greatly relieved that he was able to spek to Ana. Felipe eyed Maggie sceptically and spoke as little as possible. He was a man of few words in any case, Maggie noted. His few words about her were always scathing, however. He didn't act much like a man who was expecting a favour, and if it weren't for Ana he certainly wouldn't get one. No doubt he had said she was beautiful to coax Ana into being friendly with her.

He was in the hall next morning as Maggie came downstairs, and at the sight of her he walked forward to watch her descent. He stood at the bottom of the steps and looked up at her so fiercely that she stopped halfway down and felt quite uneasy, wondering exactly what she had done wrong.

'Don't you have any legs?' he suddenly rasped, his hands on his lean hips, his black eyes running over her in exasperation. 'Surely there must be normal feminine legs inside those masculine trousers? Everybody has them and *something* must be holding you at a given height above the ground!'

Maggie was completely open-mouthed. Nobody had ever dared to speak to her like that before. This man was either furiously insulting or dangerously mad.

'How dare you make personal remarks?' she raged, glaring down at him. 'You have no right to——'

'Indeed I have not,' he interrupted drily. 'My own courage astonishes me, and all because of foolish speculation. Naturally you have no legs. You would consider them to be a sign of weakness!'

He strode off and Maggie was so angry that she went back to her room and missed breakfast. When she went out later she was too annoyed to do anything at all but roam around fuming. Ana seemed to pick up the vibes very quickly and tagged along with Mitch, laughing at his humour, turning her head from time to time in Maggie's direction as if she could hear steam coming from her ears.

'Have I offended you, Maggie?' she asked quietly as Mitch went off to climb quite dangerously to get a shot.

'Of course not,' Maggie said quickly. 'It's just that. . .well. . .your brother annoyed me.'

'Oh! He has a very bad temper,' Ana informed her, laughing and obviously relaxing again. 'Felipe can rage like the *tormenta*. He is not like Señor Mitchell. The *señor* is gentle and kind.'

Maggie gave her a startled look. This could be the beginning of big, big trouble.

'He's very popular,' she said firmly. 'Don't you have friends of your own?'

'I have plenty of friends and sometimes they visit me here. Felipe takes me to the coast too but it is a bit difficult now that I cannot see. I know the hacienda and can be independent. On the coast it is not easy with so much traffic and so many people.'

'Yes. I expect it is,' Maggie mused. On the face of it, it seemed that she was gaining Ana's confidence, but then Felipe already had her confidence and he knew nothing at all about her blindness. Being agony aunt was tricky and probably quite beyond her.

She was still quietly fuming about Felipe's remarks as dinner drew near, however, and he had put her in a very awkward position. If she went down in trousers he would give one of those sardonic smiles. If she wore a skirt he would think she cared what he thought. It had to be one or the other unless she was prepared to sit up here, miss dinner and sulk.

After due consideration she decided to go from the sublime to the ridiculous. She had brought a couple of dresses with her because she had not been too sure

about the heat. She had not worn either of them before
and they were two years old, dresses she had bought
before events had changed her from a very easygoing,
happy person into a creature armed for defence. She got
them out and surveyed them thoughtfully.

In the end, and not without great misgivings, she
decided to wear a voile dress printed with blue and gold
flowers. It was wispy and very feminine, a dress she had
bought for a party that had in the event been missed by
at least three months. The underslip was pale blue and
around this the dress swirled like gossamer. It was only
when she had it on that she realised the danger of this.
At the sight of herself in the mirror, an image of herself
from so long ago, all the shock came back, taking her by
surprise.

She looked down at hands that trembled and for a
moment she considered taking the dress off and forgetting the whole idea. She would not, though. What had
happened to her? Had she imprisoned herself as Ana
had done? Was Felipe right about hiding? Did she hide
behind aggression and trousers as Ana hid behind eyes
that refused to see?

It was time to look the world in the face with her own
image. She would still be the same whatever she wore.
She brushed her hair and left it long and gleaming,
slipped into dainty sandals and went downstairs. If she
could face Felipe de Santis she could face anybody.

# CHAPTER FOUR

FELIPE wasn't there and Maggie experienced a great deal of cowardly relief. Mitch gave a gasp that had Ana turning questioningly to the doorway as she entered.

'Even if you attack me, Maggie, I'm going to say that you look beautiful.' He looked so serious that Maggie couldn't think of a thing to say. In any case, she was filled with anxiety about seeing the count.

'Does she?' Ana for the first time showed frustration at not being able to see. 'Tell me exactly how she looks. You are so good at describing things. It is like looking through your camera. Come and describe Maggie to me while I get her a drink.'

They were across the room when Felipe came in, and Maggie was standing alone. She had never felt so vulnerable, not for two years. She hadn't even had the nerve to glare at Mitch when he had eyed her so appreciatively. If she went on like this then she was going to have trouble when she got back to London.

Felipe stopped in the doorway, his eyes running over her slowly, lingering on her legs, her slender arms and the shining length of her hair. There was a glittering look in those dark eyes but his lips had a very sardonic twist and she knew he was about to make some scathing comment.

'Don't say anything!' she snapped, keeping her voice low and hoping that nobody else could hear. 'Just don't say a thing!'

'Am I not allowed to say *buenas tardes*?' He stopped in front of her and looked down at her from what appeared just then to be a very great height. 'I did not intend to say anything else.'

He had been! She was not at all deceived.

'You think I've done it because of what you said!' Maggie accused, her cheeks flushing.

'You cannot read my mind.' He kept his voice low as if they were conspirators and that annoyed her too. 'You have probably done it because it is hot tonight, or maybe you have used up the trousers.' He shrugged, his lips quirking. 'A woman does not have to explain why she does things. It is part of the advantage of being a woman, one of the perks. Remember that, *señorita*.' He looked across at the other two, who were laughing and taking a long time to get Maggie's drink.

'Ana has improved, relaxed,' he observed, changing the subject abruptly as if he had tired of the whole thing. 'She talks to you a great deal.'

'But not about her problem.' Maggie was thankful that her heart had settled down a bit and was not now hammering in her chest like a wild bird. It was a relief to have those dark eyes turned in another direction. Even so, his rather disdainful dismissal of her protests irritated.

'It is too soon for that. The problem goes too deep. No matter, there is plenty of time.'

'There's not!' Being here was changing her too and she couldn't hide behind the sierras for months on end. 'We can't stay here indefinitely. I'm supposed to be writing a feature, not a book.'

'There is time,' he murmured, not even looking at her, his eyes still on his sister. 'We probably need you more than they do. We will report you missing and they will forget all about you after a while. All this was Señor Parnham's idea and he will agree to almost anything I ask, as I am sure you know already.'

He just walked off and Maggie watched him worriedly. She sincerely hoped he was joking. You never could tell with Felipe de Santis and at the moment things were just as he wanted them. His attitude said he was letting her play at being a psychiatrist to please his godfather. He wasn't taking anything seriously other than treating them both as nuisances. She was dancing to his tune a little too, and she was uneasily aware of it. He was getting all his own way with very few orders. It might be very subtle but it was there. She wasn't in charge of anything.

In the sunlight of the next morning Maggie decided to go off by herself and think it all out. She had spent some time after breakfast standing on her balcony and looking out towards the mountains. To be here in Spain and not see things at close quarters was a great waste of such beauty, and she had no intention of asking Mitch to tag along either. This was her idea and it was her time. She gave herself the morning off and left the hacienda.

It was ridiculously easy to get away and her own skill brought a grin to her face. The great Felipe had not even been around and the servants had ignored the fact that the *inglésa* was calmly walking towards the great gates. Maybe they thought she was just exploring the area within the walls. She was dressed in dark jeans and a T-shirt, the usual loose shirt flung over her shoulders, and she knew her white trainers would make walking easy.

The relief as she left the place and walked along the track that led away from the Hacienda de Nieve was astounding. She had been tense since she had arrived and she knew perfectly well where all the tension was coming from — *el conde*! She couldn't even glance at him without feeling a little strange, and he never had any pleasant look on his face. He seemed to have three expressions only — sardonic, disdainful and furious. He was as tricky in his own way as any dictator she had struggled to interview. But then, he *was* a dictator. He never hesitated to dictate to her. It was good to be able to put him well behind her.

The distance was greater than she had expected. From the hacienda and from the lovely view that her balcony gave of the mountains they had seemed quite close. On foot, she realised that the astonishing light made things seem much closer than they actually were. She had come a long way and as far as she could see it would take much longer even to reach the foothills.

The sky was a remarkable shade of blue, not one cloud in sight, and as she looked up Maggie had a sudden feeling of deep peace, as if she was part of the land, knee-deep in it. It was a tranquil feeling but she also knew a strange sadness. It was a long time since she had really belonged anywhere. There was her job and her real liking for it, but in actual fact she never quite relaxed, never let her guard down.

She hardly remembered her parents, hardly remembered home. There had been her grandfather, university, her job and her flat. This was the first time she had ever honestly assessed her life. But the high mountains pulled her, the warm wind blew her long, shining hair. It whistled around her ears like mysterious music, blotting out all other sound.

Above her, an eagle soared, its gliding majesty holding her spellbound, and she was lost in a world of her own, a world she had never stepped into before as the beauty, the staggering grandeur and the warmth of Spain gripped her imagination.

The Land Rover was almost upon her before she heard the throbbing engine, and she spun round partly in a daze and certainly angered. Civilisation was encroaching on her dreamy state and she resented it. Her resentment grew as she recognised the driver. Felipe de Santis sat at the wheel, his eyes dark and irritated as he approached at speed over the rough ground. She had long since left the path and he had been travelling across rough land for some time — there was a high trail of dust behind the vehicle.

Maggie knew he was coming to get her and she was furious. He looked equally enraged. His black hair was tousled, blown by the wind, shining strands of it across his brown forehead. His hands gripped the wheel with what she took to be more than necessary strength and he looked as if he would stop, spring out and grip her neck with equal intensity.

He roared up beside her and ground to a halt, the silence after the noise of the engine actually quite frightening, and he was out of the Land Rover and towering above her before she could even open her mouth.

'Where do you imagine you are going?' He rasped out the words and stood with his hands on his hips to glare down at her. There it was again, the dictatorial attitude, and Maggie's grey eyes glared back.

'I'm walking!' She had no intention of saying anything else; in fact she had been quite undecided about answering him at all, but he looked just a bit too angry for outright defiance and he was decidedly bigger than she was.

'*Walking*? Walking into the mountains?' He glared even more, his voice harshly condemning. 'You have no water, no proper shoes. It is wild up there! The sierras are not the rolling hills of England! Is this how you conduct your life? It is a miracle you have survived. No doubt you drag Señor Mitchell about with you to carry your belongings and get you out of scrapes. I did not realise until now that he had more than one function. As a lover he is sadly lacking, *señorita*. He is not devoted enough to keep his mind strictly on you.'

Maggie went wild. The wind was blowing her hair all about her. It swirled across her furious face and she raised her voice to an actual shout.

'How dare you suggest that Mitch and I —— ?'

'I have keen eyesight,' he interrupted harshly. 'I do not actually need the evidence of two people in one bedroom and the sight of crumpled covers to point me in the right direction. I remember your determination to bring him to Spain with you.'

'He's my photographer!' Maggie yelled, grabbing at her hair and pushing the swirling strands off her face

furiously. 'I'd also seen *you*! It seemed a good idea to
have a companion when I knew I had to face a Spanish
maniac!'

For a second he looked as if he was about to grab her
and shake her to pieces, but her wild looks and her
uncontrolled temper suddenly had his lips quirking. The
haughty face was still for a second more and then he
began to laugh softly, warm, dark laughter that took her
completely by surprise.

'Get in.' He grasped her arm and nodded towards the
Land Rover, but Maggie was not about to meekly
capitulate and go back to the hacienda like an escaped
convict recaptured.

'I'm going into the mountains and don't you dare
manhandle me!' she snapped.

It amused him even more and he looked down at her
quizzically as she wrenched her arm from his grasp.

'I am not about to stop you. I will escort you and see
that you return safely.'

'I prefer to be alone!'

This announcement gained her a very wry glance and
she fumed more as she read his looks. He was thinking
of Mitch again and Maggie felt almost tongue-tied with
frustration. She was *not* going to start explaining herself
to this arrogant Spaniard. He never gave her the chance.
The hard hand captured her arm again and he turned
her to the vehicle whether she wanted to go or not.

'You are my guest, I am responsible for your safety.
You wish to see the mountains at close quarters? *Muy
bien*! I will take you. You will have more time, be able
to go further and see more. You will also be safe.'

She didn't know about safe, not with Felipe de Santis.
She might feel compelled to attack him physically at
any moment and he was alarming enough to convince
her that he would lift her in the air, shake her like a rag
doll and toss her over a crag. She went, reluctantly and
ungraciously, wrenching her arm away again. She
climbed in and he stood looking up at her ironically.

'You intend to drive, *señorita*?'

'Of course not!' she snapped at him and glared down and he smiled in a very self-satisfied manner.

'Then move over, *por favor*. In Spain we drive on the other side.' She only realised then that she was sitting behind the wheel and her flushed face flushed even further as she moved across with great difficulty. He had won again, won hands down. She sat stiffly and glared out in front of her. Everything was spoiled. Her magical feelings had quite gone and now she didn't feel knee-deep in anything but annoyance.

He set off, more slowly this time, but all the same she was being tossed about on the seat. Walking was better and she didn't want him here in any case. She was about to turn to him and demand to be taken back when he suddenly swung on to a track she had not seen from the distance. It was only wide enough for one vehicle but it was not so rough, and Maggie took a few deep breaths to get control of her rage. It was quite simple really — she wouldn't speak to him. He was wasting his morning and he could do it in silence.

With this pleasing thought she settled more comfortably and looked about her. They were climbing quite rapidly and soon Maggie's eyes took on a very troubled look. It was all right walking in the mountains but not quite so safe-looking to drive. The land was falling away to the side — *her* side! Already there was a very steep drop and as she looked up her heart slmost stopped. As far as she could see, the road was going into the sky!

Not for anything would she have informed him how much this worried her. She wasn't used to mountains and heights were always a little alarming, especially when you had a very lively imagination. She broke her vow of silence a bit desperately, though, after a few more minutes.

'Are we going up there?'

'*Sí*. It is very pleasant on the other side of the ridge. You will have good views.'

'I — I hadn't intended to come so far.'

'I am glad to hear it. However, with the Land Rover we can go as far as you want.'

Maggie wanted to say that she only wished to go back, preferably on foot, but by now words were a little difficult to utter. A quick glance at him showed her that he thought nothing at all of a drive like this, clinging to the mountainside and driving much too fast. The wheels caught loose stones and they rattled downwards to oblivion, and Maggie was sure that she would soon follow them.

'Please can we go back?' Shakily she gave in and begged, and he glanced across at her swiftly, surprise in his dark eyes.

'Something is wrong? *Qué hay?*' To her relief he stopped and she felt just a touch safer. His eyes ran over her suddenly pale face, noting the fine film of moisture on her forehead. 'You are afraid of heights?'

'Normally, no. But. . .' She glanced at the road ahead, a road that seemed to just shoot upwards at a terrifying angle. Her hands were actually shaking and she would not have believed she could have got herself into this sort of state so quickly.

'I will turn and go back.' He made a move to start the engine but Maggie was so scared that she gripped his arm, quite forgetting who he was.

'There's a place up here to turn?'

'No special place. The road is like this to the top. However, I can turn here.'

'*No!*' The idea of turning on this narrow track frightened her even more. There was no room to turn. They would go over the edge.

'You are quite safe.' He looked at her intently and she assumed he was trying to give her courage. 'People use this road. I do not ever recall an accident. I will do whatever you say.'

'We — we'll go on,' Maggie decided unsteadily, closing her eyes. The top must be at least a mile high; just how well would a four-wheel drive hold on it? She heard the engine start and they moved forwards. This time he went slowly but Maggie kept her eyes tightly closed. It was a long time since she had felt fear and it was not at all exhilarating. She didn't even grip the seat — her hands were shaking too much. By the time they got to the top she was dangerously close to tears.

Felipe stopped again and Maggie made herself look, the weakness of sheer relief flooding through her. They were off the road, parked on a wide area of land that overlooked the next valley. It was clearly a spot height — in fact there was a small stone to mark it, but it was almost hidden in rough grass and gorse, and Maggie really didn't want to know how far they had climbed.

He got out and came round to open her door.

'Step outside into the breeze,' he advised quietly. 'The road is wide from here onwards.' She didn't point out that they had to go back the way they had come, and when he reached into the back and handed her a water container she drank gladly.

'Come and look at the scene.' He took her arm and Maggie went forward slowly. Her legs were still trembling but she was pulling herself together as quickly as she could and she had to admit that his quiet actions helped.

There was a spectacular view, a green secluded valley with the mountains towering all around. She could see houses and a church. From here it looked like a toy village sparkling in the sun and on the green slopes there were sheep, a dog racing among them. She could just make out the shepherd resting beneath a tree, and the tranquillity of the scene helped to make her feel less frantic.

'*Vámonos!*' After a minute, Felipe took her arm again and she was glad to see a metalled road leading downwards. They were going to the village. At least it would give her more time to recover.

There was a small bar quite close to the church and when they arrived Felipe urged her out.

'Time for tapas.' She knew the Spanish liking for these little snacks and she stepped down into the street, a little surprised to find herself the focus of several pairs of eyes. She made a grab for her shirt but Felipe took it from her and flung it into the back. 'It is too hot. Come. Nobody is about to eat you. They are merely curious. Visitors are a rarity here.'

'They're not staring at you,' she muttered, and he suddenly grinned, quite unexpectedly.

'I have the same black hair, the same dark eyes as all the other people here. I am Andaluz. In any case, they know me.' Of course they would! He was *el conde*, probably much revered here in the mountains. She glanced at him and found his eyes steadily on her face. 'You are a novelty with your dark red hair and your grey eyes. See that they do not sparkle with anger and disappoint them.'

Maggie was still not in any condition to argue and she found herself following him to the dark little bar, almost running a gauntlet of greetings from the men standing around. She wasn't sure if she should go in there. This looked like a very male occasion but she was greeted with smiles and urged indoors where Felipe found a seat for her after she had chosen her snack from the plates on the counter.

She chose *tortilla a la española*, Spanish omelette. There were several kinds with onion, ham, asparagus, spinach and mushroom, and Maggie looked at them with glee. It seemed a long time since the small breakfast that was served in Spain, and in the end Felipe put a portion of each on her plate.

'Try the *calamares*,' he suggested, pointing to the rings fried in batter. Maggie nearly jumped out of her skin. She knew what *calamares* was — it was squid!

'No, thank you,' she managed hastily. 'You've already

filled my plate up. Anyway, I — I don't like the look of it.'

He gave her a look of amused speculation and she was glad to sit in her corner and leave him to get the drinks. She had nearly given the game away there.

The bar seemed to serve other functions besides serving drinks. Behind the long counter there were hams hanging, the smell of them adding to the already aromatic air of the place. It was a little dark after the strong sunlight, but it was cool, and she sank to her seat thankfully as Felipe stayed at the bar.

She couldn't help watching him. Right now, after her ordeal, she was shaken out of antagonism. He was still as magnificent-looking as he had been when she was a child. He was tall, hard, handsome with the flashing good looks of the people of Andalucía. Their Moorish ancestry was still visible, not only in the land but in the tilt of the head, the hard, sensuous lips, the quick glitter of their eyes, and she had to admit that Felipe de Santis was a prince among them.

Not that he behaved like one here. He reserved that for her. He collected their drinks and turned from the bar where he had been at the centre of a laughing group of men who frequently glanced at her curiously.

'*Su mujer es muy guapa, Señor Conde*,' a man said with a grin. '*Una paloma*.'

Felipe shot a quick glance at her, his eyes flashing over her, and Maggie tried hard to look normal and unenlightened.

'What did he say?' she asked as Felipe sat down next to her.

'Obviously he noticed your grey eyes. So far they have not hardened to ice. He called you a dove — *una paloma*.' His lips twisted wryly. 'Do not be alarmed. They are not uncivilised people. It was a compliment.'

The man had said more than that. He had said she was beautiful and called her Felipe's woman, but obviously the count was not about to enlighten her on that particular score, and as she was not revealing her knowledge of his language she had to let it go. It would have been a little more civilised if he had pointed out that she was a guest at the hacienda, instead of sitting here with that look on his face.

She was grateful for the cool drink, however, and for the really tasty snack. It put a bit of life back into her and she was able to leave with more dignity than she had felt on arrival as Felipe politely held her chair and said *adiós* to the still intrigued customers.

'There is another way back,' he said quietly as Maggie stood by the Land Rover and cast a rather fearful eye up the valley.

'Oh! Thank you!' She blurted it out quite innocently and he stood and looked down at her upturned face.

'I am not cruel, *señorita*.' His brown hand tilted her face. 'I do not like to see fear in a woman's eyes, especially a woman who places so much value in equality. We will battle with each other on safe, neutral ground, *sí*?'

'It's not exactly neutral at the hacienda,' Maggie pointed out. He was making her feel a bit strange again with his hand on her skin and she was at a decided disadvantage. It seemed unworthy to snatch her face away and glare when he had treated her so well. 'You're in complete charge and you resent me anyway.'

'Do I?' His black brows rose quizzically. 'Surely you realise your power, *señorita*? I need your help.'

'Not really,' Maggie protested. 'Any woman would do if you imagine that's what you need.'

He grinned down at her and it was only then that she realised just what she had said.

'A very ambiguous statement,' he murmured in amusement. 'However, I will let it pass. You must still be in shock. As to any woman being suitable for Ana's needs, I think not. In any case, I am stuck with you, *es verdad*?'

A slight sparkle came to Maggie's eyes and he recognised the signs of growing annoyance. His hand slid from her face to her shoulder and he glanced towards the bar where the men had brought their drinks out to see the very last of this unusual event.

'Let us go, *señorita*,' Felipe advised quietly. 'So far they are impressed by your beauty and your grace. We will leave while you are still in control of that temper. Let them go on thinking of you as *una paloma*. When we are home you can once again be a fiery dragon.'

She didn't say anything. For a start, there was the road to face, and for another she didn't make scenes in public. They left in a cloud of dust and shouted farewells but Maggie absolutely refused to smile. She was not about to confirm their obvious belief that the count had found himself a new woman.

The road back was easy and she had the chance to look around. Felipe drove in silence and they were soon back — a fact that brought a slight tinge of regret to her face. In the silence of the return journey she had almost slipped back to tranquillity and, oddly enough, it had helped to have him there beside her.

Maggie realised that she felt perfectly safe with him. In spite of his arrogance, his derisive remarks and his sardonic glances, he had the generosity of all Spaniards. He was naturally courteous, reliable. Somehow he made her feel that she belonged. It was a long time since she had felt that.

She was surprised to find that it was still not too late, only lunchtime actually, and she was further surprised when Felipe merely informed the other two that they had been driving in the mountains. He said nothing at all about his angry chase after her and nothing about her fear. He never even looked at her. She might very well have just arrived for all the notice he took of her.

The slight warmth was absolutely gone as if it had never been. He was a very odd man, she decided, and very annoying. It annoyed her even more that his continuing aristocratic demeanour disappointed her after the way she had been thinking about him. Still, what did she expect? He had said that he was stuck with her. She decided to get right on with her article and also to seek Ana out and make a friend of her. She had to get out of here as soon as possible. She was very determined about survival, especially her own.

Next morning Maggie found Ana in the pool. This would be a very good chance to get more friendly still. It was hot, sunny and the water looked so cool and inviting that Maggie felt quite downcast about having no swimsuit. She didn't much feel like sitting beside the pool and simply shouting to Ana. It was no use trying to borrow one — Ana was much smaller, nowhere near to Maggie's slender height. There was only one way to get one and that was to go and buy one. Maggie was quite astonished at her own determination on that score. The old Maggie would have shrugged and gone without. The old Maggie would not have even thought about it in the first place.

There being only one way to get out of here, she went to find Felipe. She knew where he would be straight after breakfast. He would be with the horses, either in one of the fenced enclosures or in one of the stables. She hoped he had not gone to the further fields. Having become impatient, she would not take well to any delay.

She could see him long before she reached him. He was in one of the enclosures with the horses. They were beautiful, these Andalucían horses, and she had been given a long lecture on the subject by Ana, who seemed to be an expert. She knew they were a light-saddle horse with a good disposition in spite of the spirited, fiery temperament. All she could see, however, was their beauty. Some were white and some grey, their eyes large and flashing. The long, flowing manes and tails were like silk and their high-stepping stately walk was a delight to watch.

He was leading one out as she reached him and he never stopped. He just looked at her very comprehensively, his eyes roaming over her, and then he nodded politely and led the horse away. Maggie was a bit shaken at his silence and knew she was once again blushing. This morning she had fought a battle with herself and had left off the concealing shirt. She was wearing jeans but her top was a rather tight yellow T-shirt and she felt as gauche as a schoolgirl and very vulnerable.

'I want to talk to you,' she managed firmly, having to walk fast to keep up with him.

'*Muy bien.* I am listening.' He led the horse into one of the stables and the shock after the bright light made Maggie blink for a few seconds. By the time she had herself sorted out the animal was standing like a rock and Felipe was grooming it steadily and expertly. He never looked at her and she had the feeling that she should be hopping about from one foot to the next, ready to beg. There was no doubt in her mind that he was doing this deliberately and it drove her to forcefulness.

'I want to go to town—any town,' she said determinedly. 'It doesn't have to be big; all it has to have is a good shop or two.'

'Indeed.' He just went on with his task, his eyes on the horse, his strong brown hand working methodically. 'I suppose it must also have a public telephone that can be used in private and a post office that will send out mail? You know the rules. Neither of you can leave here until I have seen the photographs and the writing.'

'If we were close to a town I wouldn't even inform you,' Maggie said evenly, the desire to needle him coming out of nowhere. 'I'd just ring a taxi. The only reason for this conversation is that I need transport.'

She leaned back against the wall and looked at him tauntingly as his head rose sharply at her tone and his eyes fastened on her.

'And what has a town got to offer that the hacienda cannot?' He stood quite still now, watching her, and she didn't feel quite so bold with his eyes narrowed on her intently, suspicious but interested. His gaze left her face and began to roam over her figure, and her nerve gave out entirely.

'I want to buy a swimsuit. I never expected it to be so hot at this time of the year and I didn't know there was a pool. With a swimsuit I can swim with Ana and get to know her better. Jorge can take me,' she finished in a wild rush as his eyes stopped at her breasts and lingered unforgivably, making her hot and anxious.

'No.' He simply went back to the grooming and she could hardly believe it.

'What do you mean, no? I refuse to be a prisoner!'

'You are not. Jorge cannot take you. I will take you myself—tomorrow.'

'I want to go *now*!'

She felt childishly petulant as soon as she said it, and he looked at her wryly, putting the brush down and coming to stand in front of her. His sleeves were rolled up, his dark hair had fallen partly across his forehead, and Maggie suddenly realised he was dangerously attractive besides every other danger he represented.

'You said that like a spoiled little girl, *señorita*, and not like an icy journalist at all.' His hands came down at either side of her, trapping her against the wall. 'Your trip to Spain is changing you already.'

He stood looking down at her and Maggie felt waves of anxiety wash over her. She had lost her fear long ago but she had not been close to a man like this for over two years. She had no idea what to do; somehow fighting was not the right thing at this moment. She would feel ridiculous because he would simply show that ironic, arrogant surprise if she panicked.

He moved one hand and tilted her face.

'You are afraid to be a woman.'

'I'm not afraid of anything!' Maggie assured him, struggling back into her old character almost frantically.

'You are afraid of me.' He looked down at her steadily and Maggie tried to stay cool, but she was losing this battle and she knew it.

'I'm not!' Even to her own ears the denial sounded weak, and he smiled grimly.

'We will see.'

# CHAPTER FIVE

BEFORE Maggie could move, Felipe's hand slid behind her head, beneath her hair, and he pulled her towards him fast, his dark head bending, his mouth closing over hers determinedly. She was too frightened to struggle. It was all very well beating a man at his own game when she was standing free and able to lash out with her acid tongue. Now, though, she was even powerless to move, although he did not attempt to draw her against him.

His hand held her head up, his lips held her spellbound. She had not been kissed for over two years and it was magical; she was feeling it deeply, listening with everything in her but not remembering, because other kisses had not been like this. It made her warm, relaxed, and she didn't try to escape. It was like the sun coming out after a long time of darkness.

He lifted his head and looked down at her, his hand still cupping her face. 'How innocent you seem,' he murmured derisively, 'and how very sensuous — a woman after all.'

'You — you know nothing about me,' Maggie said shakily.

'I am a man, *señorita*. You're eyes are very expressive and so is your reaction . You are very much a woman.'

'You had no right to do that,' Maggie whispered, still not enough in control of herself to be outraged. 'You have no right to speak like that either. I'll — leave here.'

'How will you leave if I do not let you?' He looked down at her imperiously. 'What was it after all but an experiment? Your reaction was not exactly innocent in spite of your looks.'

'I'm a guest. You had no right to — to kiss me.'

Maggie was feeling more frantic by the second. She knew exactly how she had reacted and she had no explanation for it, not even one to offer herself.

'I did not kiss you,' he said softly. 'I was merely calming a spoiled child. *This* is a kiss, *señorita*.'

This time his arms wrapped around her, pulling her to the hard, strong warmth of his body, his hand bringing her face close again. The lips that had soothed now hardened, and when she stiffened in fright his tongue ran along her mouth with shocking intimacy, easing her lips apart and moving inside to tease her tongue and explore the warmth.

Maggie gave a low moan, her knees sagging, and he caught her close, turning her head to his shoulder, deepening the kiss and holding her against the length of his body. Heat flooded down to her toes, her hands went limp and she completely forgot where she was. She had no judgement, no memory, only a growing hunger and a quickly mounting pain she had never felt before. Her breasts tightened painfully and he pulled her closer as if he knew, his kiss deepening further.

The horse made a small fretful sound and Felipe raised his head.

'I think, like a woman, she is jealous,' he said with a quizzical look. He ran his hand down Maggie's flushed cheek. 'In ten minutes I will be finished here. Come riding with me.'

'No!' Maggie's legs came to life, although shakily, and she sprang away.

'You cannot ride? It does not matter. These horses have a superb disposition in spite of their high spirits. You will not be tossed off.'

'It's not the horse I'm suspicious of,' Maggie snapped, getting her own spirit back.

'You imagine I will seduce you?' He went back to his task, his smile scathing. 'It is my intention to take Ana riding too. I am not about to find a secluded spot and continue your lesson.'

'It wasn't a lesson, it was an unforgivable action!'

'Had I continued the action you would have been even more willing by now.' He glanced up, his gaze roaming over her flushed face and wildly grey eyes. There was nothing she could do to disguise the swift rise and fall of her breasts and his eyes rested there before returning to capture her own gaze. 'Obviously you are not seeing enough of Señor Mitchell. You need someone to make love to you. I am not offering. I am merely your psychiatrist, *señorita*.' He gave her a very mocking bow, his smile gleaming white and taunting against a tanned face, and Maggie fled, ignoring his final instructions to put on some sensible shoes and tell Ana.

She would do no such thing. She ran to the house and up to her room, the swimsuit forgotten, and she shut the door tightly. It was unbelievable — not only that he had done it but that she had stood there and let him. He imagined he could act like this. It was inexcusable! Nobody had ever dared to do anything like that before. She was Maggie Howard, secure and safe in her job and her way of life.

She sat down to rage silently but in spite of every effort to work herself up rage would not come and honesty forced her to face facts. It had been magical, filling her with hunger and crumbling her shell to dust. There was no pearl inside, though, nothing nearly so hard and polished. There was just a trembling being as vulnerable as any other woman, a being who had craved much, much more. He surely could not have known that in spite of his final words. He had called her sensuous. All she could do was hide.

It was not allowed. Nothing was allowed unless Felipe allowed it, and Ana came to her room some twenty minutes later, all dressed for riding.

'Felipe says we are all waiting for you,' she told Maggie quickly. 'He says that the ride will clear your headache away.'

Maggie fumed. He had considered her probable

excuse and dispatched it swiftly. He was showing her that she was under his thumb. Well, she would go and she would ignore him.

'Is Mitch going too?'

'Yes. He is going to take some photographs. He will photograph me on the horse and I will have it to keep. He says so.'

Maggie was sure he meant it too. The reason for being here was disappearing more each day. He had been told to take photographs for the magazine, not to give to Ana. No doubt the other shots of Ana would end up beside Mitch's bed. If Felipe de Santis had his eyes on his sister a little more he would see what was happening. Complications were growing and she was no further forward with her task. She had no idea why Ana was blind, and there wasn't a feature in sight. Maggie hadn't even taken notes, and most of Mitch's shots seemed to be for pleasure.

She found the most sensible shoes she had and prepared to depart, rushing back at the last minute to snatch up a loose shirt and shrug into it. Better to be hot than visible. Her only problem now was how to face Felipe, because she was quite sure that he would not be embarrassed. Any feelings present would be her own, but she was determined not to show them.

He wasn't embarrassed. He looked at her with sardonic amusement which deepened when she quickly looked away. The others were already mounted and Maggie felt herself begin to tremble as Felipe came up and prepared to help her.

'*Tranquilo*,' he advised drily. 'It is perfectly natural to enjoy being kissed.'

'I did not enjoy it!' Maggie spat, alarmed that the others might hear and wishing she did not have to speak to him at all.

'You did and so did I.' He looked up at her when she was seated on a calm grey horse. 'Allow yourself to be a woman. It is useless to struggle against it. For you it is inevitable—you are beautiful and desirable. There is passion in you. The shirt does not protect you, it merely hints at secrets. You will find it more comfortable to be what you are.'

'I'm a well-paid, respected journalist. I know what I am!' Maggie snapped in a low voice, her cheeks wildly pink.

'So do I,' he stated derisively. 'That is why I kissed you, *señorita.*'

What exactly did he mean by that? She opened her mouth to demand an explanation but he simply walked away and swung easily into the saddle, his black hair glinting in the sunlight, and Maggie had to drag her eyes from him. She couldn't seem to stop watching him. In spite of her rage with him she admitted that she found him just about perfect to look at. It was like waking up after a long, long nightmare, but it was not safe at all to be awake.

Ana had no trouble with her mount; to Maggie's surprise she seemed to be an expert horsewoman and Mitch too seemed to take to the activity like a veteran. Maggie never gave a thought to hers. It seemed to adapt itself to her and, in any case, she would not have noticed if it had been a giraffe. Her mind was too much in a whirl and she searched rather frantically for her old self. The speed with which she had changed and was continuing to change was frightening. Deep inside she knew she should leave here and go back to England as quickly as possible before all her defences collapsed.

*El conde* hovered over his kingdom like an eagle, sharp-eyed and cold, ready to swoop at any moment. She had relaxed her hard grip on life in this beautiful, tranquil place and he had swooped on her—unforgivably. At this rate she would not be the same. She would be afraid again and the people would see her vulnerability.

Felipe reined back and came to ride beside her, a rather tight look on his face, and she soon found out why.

'I will take you to the shops tomorrow morning, *señorita*,' he informed her grimly. 'I have promised. Perhaps you can assist me too by pointing out to your companion that Ana is to be left alone and not inveigled into — friendship. I do not relish the thought of leaving her here with him while I drive you for many miles and wait for you to linger by shop windows.'

Maggie's heart sank. So he had noticed how close Mitch and Ana were getting. She might have known. She had noticed herself and Felipe de Santis didn't miss anything at all.

'Surely she'll want to come too?'

'You are very much mistaken,' he muttered, looking beyond them and keeping a close eye on his sister and Mitch as they rode along laughing and talking. 'My sister is not quite as docile as you seem to think. I have invited her to join us. Her answer was a swift and unequivocal no. I have few doubts as to why.'

'Jorge can take me,' Maggie said, feeling an incredible little burst of disappointment that Felipe would not be driving her.

'No!' he said adamantly. 'I take you. I have no intention of letting you out of my sight.'

Maggie felt annoyance mounting. It would be easy enough to let this go in view of his problem, but she refused to be dictated to in any way at all.

'It's no use whatever telling you that Mitch is reliable and trustworthy, is it?' Maggie asked irritably. He thought the worst of Mitch and clearly thought that left to herself she would ring London at once. He was making her feel defenceless and then striking at her.

'It is not. He is obviously intent upon amusing himself with two women. Either that or he is doing this with deliberate skill to gain her confidence.'

'To what purpose?' Maggie turned her head to glare at him and he looked straight back at her coldly, none of the sexual speculation in his glance.

'To pry into our lives, *señorita*. As to your trip, Jorge

would be very easy to fool. Already he goes in awe of you. One call to London and we would have hordes of the Press at the gates of the hacienda, the headlines already written: "Ana de Santis Blind".'

'You're judging me by your own standards!' Maggie accused furiously, not one bit embarrassed now. 'I like Ana. You asked me to help. You can see for yourself how gentle Mitch is with her. He likes her too and only that. If the Press were to arrive you'd find both of us at the gates with shot-guns. And another thing,' she added angrily before he could reply, 'I can't personally see why Ana should interest the Press. It must be your enlarged opinion of yourself. If it were that much of an interest and so very newsworthy I'd want the scoop myself.'

'You know who I am,' he pointed out tightly. 'I do not imagine for a minute that someone of your ability will have come here without prying into my background. It is a long time ago but still worth a story in some paper if Ana's problem can be tagged on to it.'

'I was more or less ordered out here! This is the last place I want to be and I'm not at all interested in your background. News is soon dead. I was a child when you were famous and that makes it very dead.'

'Not if they can rake something up about Ana!'

Maggie gave a great sigh of exasperation. 'Look, it's all too complicated. Forget it. I'll do without a swimsuit. It was childish to want one anyway.'

'It was not childish to want one,' he corrected, his voice suddenly wryly amused. 'It was perhaps childish to want one *now*. I will take the risk. After all, there are servants here. She will not be alone with him.'

'Mitch is not a dangerous Romeo!' Maggie snapped. 'In any case, I told you, forget it.'

'I will take you in the morning.'

Maggie shot him an impatient glance. He seemed to have changed his mind with suspicious ease, and in any case she was not at all used to this kind of treatment. She was being treated like a prisoner.

'I hope you realise you can't just keep us here, waiting for a miracle. I have a busy life and being here is interrupting it.'

'You were ordered here,' he reminded her coolly. 'I did not want you here and I certainly do not want Ana's life complicated further.'

'Then order us back!' she snapped. 'Just fly us out of here and I'll take my complication with me.'

'He can go as soon as he likes,' Felipe said grimly. 'I need you here. Ana likes you and may very well confide in you. If you wish to leave, then solve my mystery, *señorita*.'

'For goodness' sake, call me Maggie!' she advised frustratedly. 'I'm trapped, bored and choked with formality.'

She expected some fury but none was forthcoming and she glanced across at him to find his eyes were fixed on the mountains, his face sombre.

'I too tire of formality,' he confessed harshly. 'For much of my life I lived in the Hacienda de Nieve surrounded by savage formality. Before my father died I cast it all aside, lived as I imagined I wanted to live. Now I am back here and the old ways return as if I have assumed his mantle.'

She knew then that Devlin Parnham was right. Felipe blamed himself for Ana's blindness and he suffered in his own cold, imperious way.

'Ana is improving daily,' she said briskly, changing the conversation very firmly away from the past. 'She looks happy. She's delightful.'

'She was always delightful—my little sister,' he said softly.

Ana lingered to join them and Felipe evidently took this as a very good sign. He cantered off and rode beside Mitch, and Maggie hoped he was not giving out any threatening advice. Things were pretty tense as it was and all her own tension had come flooding back, especially when she thought of her reaction to Felipe.

'You are enjoying this ride, Maggie?' Ana asked softly, and Maggie took a deep breath and tried to get a smile into her voice.

'It's wonderful!'

It was. They had gone a long way without her even knowing it and they were riding beside the lake she had seen from the air. Their path, though, was high up, the lake glittering below them but Maggie was not nervous. It was not the horrendous drop that had frightened her as she rode in the Land Rover. All the same it was a long way down and she hoped that Ana did not ever come here alone.

She voiced her disquiet and Ana laughed.

'I would not dare. The lake is very deep, even to the edge. I come with Felipe. It is never alarming when he is near, although I remember the drop to the lake. Felipe is a wonderful horseman.'

'I know,' Maggie said quietly. 'I remember him from a long time ago. Felipe de Santis of Spain. Nobody could ever forget him. He must have loved doing that wonderful Spanish riding.'

'Loved? I am not sure. Perhaps he did finally but originally it was merely to defeat my father.' There was something in Ana's voice that held Maggie silent. She had the tremendous feeling that Ana was speaking almost against her will, as if the words were being torn from her. When Maggie glanced across, Ana's face was strained and pale. She said nothing and was surprised whne Ana continued with no prompting at all.

'Our father was very strict, Spanish nobility at its most severe, and this place did not ring with laughter. We have much proptery, more estates and a great deal of business. Felipe was made to work very hard all the time. But he was young, filled with laughter and had ambition of his own. He was a superb horseman and in those days we had many more horses here, bloodstock that was famous as even now these horses are.

'Felipe wished to compete. He wished to ride for his country, for Spain. My father would not hear of it. A Spanish aristocrat did not compete for medals. Competition dressage was for other people — the newly rich and their daughters. The *Haute Ecole* was permissible, though. At one time the kings and princes of Europe acquired these skills and there was much training required to give the animals the necessary muscular strength. To my father it sounded very much like hard work, and that was *most* acceptable. He was sure that Felipe would give it up. He did not. He drew an irritating line between one thing and another that my father could not quite forbid. There were no medals for Felipe to win for his country but he put Spain on the map, his name on every tongue. He became famous and performed all over the world.'

'So things worked out for the best, I suppose,' Maggie said carefully. She knew from Devlin Parnham that the old count had been a hard man. He also seemed like a cruel one to her. 'Your father must have been very proud of him.'

'He would not even acknowledge the success!' Ana said bitterly. 'He refused to see Felipe perform. The whole world applauded but my father ignored it.'

'Did you see him ride?'

'Once, once only in Madrid. I was not allowed to watch again. I was sent to a boarding-school —— ' She made an angry gesture with her hand. 'Oh, not as a punishment for watching. It had been planned already. Felipe did not want me to go but my father listened to no one. I was sent there and they too were strict, severe. There was not even a television for me to watch Felipe. In the holidays I was not allowed to watch at home either.'

There was deep bitterness and something much more. Ana who was so sweet, so natural, seemed to be on the point of hysteria. Maggie glanced anxiously at Felipe but he was riding in silence with Mitch, well in front of them. It was entirely up to her.

'Well, it was a long time ago. I don't suppose anyone is strict with you now.' She turned to Ana with a smile, making herself sound calm, but she made a mistake. The horse, who had steadily been moving along in a quiet way, gave a strange little leap and she realised she had inadvertently dug her heels into his side. The action brought him close to the edge of the path. She had been so engrossed with Ana that she had paid no attention to the path and at this part it was narrow. The horse moved on to unsound ground, feeling the danger and scrabbling for a foothold. There was no foothold and Maggie gave a cry of fear as she too felt the ground give way beneath them as they slid over the edge towards the lake.

Somehow, she stayed in the saddle. It was sheer chance and not any skill at all. She heard Ana scream her name but it had all happened so fast that she was stunned. The horse still searched desperately for a footing in the soft, moving earth of the cliff-side and Maggie felt that every bone in her body was jarred as the flying hoofs found what they sought.

They landed on a ledge wide enough to hold them, the horse shivering with fear but knowing not to move at all. Maggie slid from the saddle and held the reins, her eyes on the drop to the lake. By now they were almost halfway down, the drop not so far as it had been, but it was still a long way and Maggie almost crept to the slight shelter of the rocky bank. Like the horse, she was shivering with reaction and her legs simply gave way beneath her.

'Do not move at all!' She looked up and saw Felipe lying at the top, head and shoulders over the drop, and Mitch joined him as she was still looking dazedly upwards. 'Are you hurt?' Felipe was keeping his voice as low as possible and she knew why. Her unfortunate mount was shocked enough without the sound of any loud voices. She just shook her head and went on looking up at him.

'Let the reins fall.' Felipe issued the order very calmly but she just couldn't let go.

'He — he's so close to the edge.'

'And if he falls you will go with him. Let the reins fall and move further away very carefully.'

She obeyed and he watched with still, dark eyes until she was as far as she could get from the trembling animal.

'*Muy bien*! I will get you.'

She wondered hysterically how he proposed to do that. The ledge wasn't big enough for two people and one horse, and at the moment she knew that she was incapable of helping herself. She was still gazing upwards anxiously when Felipe reappeared, and this time he was climbing down. There was a rope around his waist and he was letting himself down, hand over hand. The horse stamped anxiously as stones were dislodged, but instinct kept him still and soon Felipe was beside Maggie, both of them pressed to the edge of the cliff.

'You are not hurt?' he asked again, looking at her intently.

'No. I — I'm just shocked. I don't know how it happened.'

'*No importa*. Put your arm round my neck.' His arm came tightly around her and Maggie did exactly as he asked as she saw Mitch looking down at them. 'Ready!' Felipe ordered and the rope became taut, slowly beginning to move as Felipe started the climb back.

'You can't!' Maggie began anxiously but he never even bothered to answer. His arm tightened like iron and all she could do was cling on and try to help. They were being pulled steadily, Felipe digging his feet into the side of the cliff, and as they came to the top he eased Maggie over the edge and them came up himself.

'Oh, lord! Maggie, I thought you were a goner.' Mitch knelt beside her as she lay for a moment on the ground. 'Ana screamed and when I looked round you weren't there at all.'

'It was sheer stupidity on my part,' Maggie confessed, but Felipe looked down at her intently and shook his head.

'My stupidity. I allowed you to ride alone when I had no knowledge at all of your ability. You were close to the edge,' he added severely.

'Well, I didn't want Ana there, and in any case I — I forgot. We were talking and. . .'

The fact that she had been protecting Ana brought a flashing glance from Felipe but he did not soften at all. Instead he pulled her to her feet and watched her move.

'You seem to be unharmed,' he murmured drily. 'I am relieved to see it. I have never lost a guest yet.'

Maggie's outrage at this callous remark was somewhat offset by the fact that he had rescued her, and in any case she was moving off to Ana who was sitting looking very shaky. Felipe took no notice whatever of his sister and it was Maggie who had to comfort her and assure her that no harm had been done.

As yet, Mitch was too occupied with the rope to do more than glance in their direction. She noted that it was one of the horses who had pulled them up. Some pretty quick action had taken place and she had no doubt at all as to who had been issuing orders.

Felipe was standing on the cliff-top and looking down, and Maggie felt guilty again as belatedly she remembered the horse.

'Will you pull him up?' she asked anxiously when Felipe just stood silently and assessed the situation.

'I think not. We would have to get a special cradle to do that and I have no real idea as to how long his nerve will hold. Lower me to him,' he ordered, turning to Mitch.

The rope was once again attached to a tree and then

to the saddle of Felipe's horse, and Maggie lay back on the cliff-top to watch as he made another dangerous trip over the edge. He untied the rope and then bent, inspecting the horse carefully, examining each leg, and they could hear him talking all the time, soothing, quiet words that stilled the animal.

'Great Scott!' Mitch gasped the words and Maggie could not utter a sound as, to their astonishment, Felipe carefully mounted the horse. 'What the hell is he going to do?'

'What is it?' Ana came to the edge and Mitch just grabbed her, his arm tightly around her.

'Just keep still,' he ordered. 'We don't want you over there too. He's just inspecting the horse,' he added, glancing at Maggie with raised brows.

Maggie could hardly breathe. She had no idea what Felipe was going to do. Whatever he did it would be dangerous, and she felt her heart hammering wildly as he gathered the reins and continued with the soothing words.

He suddenly turned the horse's head, slapped hard at the quivering flanks, and Maggie felt her cheeks actually pale as the horse leapt from the ledge towards the lake, Felipe securely in the saddle. She remembered that Ana had told her it was deep right to the edge and she prayed that it was. It would be hard enough hitting water. If there was no deep water Felipe would be killed.

He somehow kept the horse in check, stilling the natural panic. It was like a wild, graceful leap in the air and they both disappeared momentarily into the deep water of the lake. It was so blue, mirroring the clear sky, and as they surfaced Maggie's heart started again and tears stung at her eyes. She had caused all this and whatever excuses Felipe had made for her she felt the guilt deeply.

'I've never seen anything like that in my life,' Mitch announced in absolute awe. 'It would have been a prize-winning shot and all I did was stand here like a fool.

Come on,' he added impatiently, 'they're swimming to
the bank further back. End of our ride, I would think.'

Maggie was glad of it; her legs felt like jelly and she
was beyond worrying if Mitch could see the tears
starting to her cheeks.

'What did he do?' Ana asked quietly. 'It is all right
now?'

'It's all right, love,' Mitch said soothingly, leading
them both to the horses. 'As to what he did, it's safe
enough to tell you now. He just got on the horse and
launched off into space, landed in the lake and he's
swimming it out.'

He sounded utterly bemused and Maggie was all of
that, to add to her other problems. Ana sighed thankfully and smiled.

'That sounds just like Felipe. He fears nothing. They
used to say that he could almost make a horse fly.'

'Well, he just did,' Mitch muttered, 'and I stood there
like an idiot, my mouth open and my camera not four
yards behind me.'

Ana started to laugh and Mitch gave her a startled
glance and then laughed ruefully too, giving her a hug.

'You're a little nuisance,' he said happily. 'As to your
brother, he's mad.'

'He is not mad at all,' Ana said cheerfully. 'He is a
Spaniard.' She was quite back to normal, proud of
Felipe and very happy. Mitch was laughing and Maggie
looked at them dolefully. They were all mad. *She* was
crying silently and she couldn't seem to stop. Felipe was
out of the water and waiting for them as they arrived at
the place where the lake quietly lapped the path.

'Bravo!' Ana called gaily as she heard him.

'Amen!' Mitch agreed with still a great deal of awe in
his voice. Maggie said nothing at all. She was trailing
behind the other two and trying to get a grip on her
nerves. She only looked up as Felipe reined in beside
her.

'I — I'm on your horse,' she murmured shakily,

wiping her eyes with the back of her hand and glancing up at him.

'He is not objecting and neither am I,' Felipe said quietly. He just rode beside her, saying nothing else, and Maggie had to speak or burst into stormy tears.

'I damned near killed you with my carelessness!' she burst out suddenly, and she was glad that he didn't even look at her.

'You did not. It was not too far to jump and I know every inch of the lake. It was merely an easy way to save a good animal. He is none the worse for it.'

'*Easy*? It was terrifying!' Maggie glared at him through eyes glazed with tears, and he shrugged, glancing a brilliant look at her that took in everything.

'It was interesting. It is years since I risked my neck. I am wet but utterly unharmed and I enjoyed it.'

'You're mad!' Maggie snapped. She was trembling like a leaf and there he was, arrogantly amused and highly self-satisfied. 'No, I forgot,' she added waspishly, 'Ana had it right. You're not mad, you're a Spaniard!'

Infuriatingly he just laughed quietly and she flatly refused to even glance at him again.

Back at the hacienda she abandoned the horses and fled to her room, leaving the others to see to them and turn them into the enclosures. She knew that in spite of his words Felipe would want to inspect the adventurous horse closely, and she wasn't going to hang about and burst into tears again.

A good shower helped, but she would have liked to go down and search for a stiff drink. She sat on the edge of the bed in her dressing-gown and towelled her hair furiously. What a catastrophe! Looking back, she couldn't remember when she had last cried — not since her terrible night so long ago. She had just gone to pieces and she had caused it all herself. Raging at Felipe had just been because she'd been shocked and scared for him when she'd seen him take off into the air.

She didn't even know herself any more. At this rate

she would go back to London a nervous wreck and have to resign. She pulled the towel over her head and had another weep—a good one this time to get it out of her system.

'*Tranquilo*. Nothing has happened that is bad. In any case, it is all over.' She had never heard anyone come in and had never expected it. Certainly she had not expected Felipe, and her tears stopped suddenly as she absorbed this new shock. 'I have brought you a brandy,' he added when she just sat there with the towel completely over her head.

Maggie looked up, peering at him, the towel like a white tent over her head, her long hair half over her face. Two grey eyes looked at him through tears and he suddenly grinned, his eyes dancing.

'Maggie Howard, you are unique,' he said with laughter in his voice. 'With you, one should expect the unexpected. Come out of your hiding place and drink the brandy.'

'I don't drink,' Magige assured him shakily, ignoring her previous thoughts of raiding his cupboards for stiff drinks.

'You will drink this, though.' He pulled her to her feet, pushed the towel to her shoulders and placed the drink firmly in her hands. 'All of it,' he added firmly when she sipped and made a face. 'It will bring you back to furious life.'

'I'm all right,' Maggie muttered, turning away.

He took her shoulders and turned her back to face him, his hand tilting her face in a very imperious manner.

'You will be when you have finished the drink. I intend to stay until you do so.'

The threat was enough to have Maggie drinking swiftly, and it went right to her head. He took the glass just in time as she swayed dizzily, and his arm caught her, lashing around her waist and holding her still.

'Rest on the bed for a while,' he advised with another

wide grin. 'By dinnertime you will be back to your old self, quite normal.'

'I'm normal now,' Maggie assured him in a fuzzy voice as he helped her to the bed and lifted her on to it.

'I am beginning to believe that,' he agreed, his dark eyes glittering with laughter. 'It has been a memorable day. I may well keep you here for your entertainment value.'

He moved the wet towel and began to straighten her hair, hovering over her like a dark-faced god, and Maggie knew she should be battling with him.

'It's not funny!' she protested vaguely.

'But you are not seeing what I see,' he assured her. 'Have a nice little sleep and all will be well.'

'You've made me drunk!' Maggie managed as he began to walk out.

'I have anaesthetised you,' he corrected drily. 'Perhaps you should be like that more often. It would keep you out of mischief.'

'You're an impossible man!' Maggie got out hazily. 'You're arrogant and impatient and chauvinistic and. . .'

'*Es verdad*,' he agreed, turning at the door to look at her wryly as her eyes closed. 'Sleep, *señorita*. It solves a lot of problems.'

It wouldn't solve anything, Maggie mused. She was an idiot, coming apart at the seams, and she hadn't written a word. What was she doing here anyway? She was asleep before an answer presented itself.

# CHAPTER SIX

NEXT morning Maggie was on her way to the shops, the hacienda left behind. She found the whole thing very embarrassing and had tried several times to back out of it, but Felipe would not hear of such a thing. Ana and Mitch had been intrigued, especially at dinner when the count had firmly called Maggie by her name. Ana had beamed at this and Mitch had looked stunned, especially as Felipe had almost choked over the necessity to say Mitch and extend the same courtesy to both his guests.

Having instigated this trip in the first place, Maggie became most anxious and cornered Mitch upstairs after breakfast.

'You're responsible for Ana today,' she warned seriously.

'Thank you. The pleasure is all mine.' He grinned at her and Maggie looked at him heatedly.

'There's to be no pleasure, just responsibility. I've taken it upon myself to assure the count that you're almost perfect. Guard Ana with your life, and I mean *your life!*'

'Damn it all, Maggie, you know I'd guard her with my life!' he said furiously. 'Just because you're wanting a cosy trip with Felipe de Santis there's no need to drag my character into it!'

'That's both impudent and unfair!' Maggie raged, her face flushing wildly.

'I've never seen you behave before as you do with him. I'm not sure if I'm not jealous.'

'Don't be ridiculous! And I don't behave. . .'

'Spur-of-the-moment pique,' he explained drily, laughing and leaning over daringly to kiss her cheek.

'You are ready, *señorita*?' The count's cold voice and his return to formality assured Maggie that he had seen this small action and now he sat beside her with a set look on his face that told her he might very well not speak for the whole of the journey.

'I am taking you to Jaén,' he announced after a few miles. 'It has more dignity than charm but it has shops and is closer than Córdoba.'

'Thank you. I'll try to hurry when we get there.' Maggie felt greatly subdued now and disappointed.

'There is no real need to hurry,' he assured her coldly. 'It will take us about an hour to get there. The distance is not too great but the roads are of questionable quality. However, I am not now so anxious about my sister being left with Señor Mitchell. Clearly, as I suspected originally, his great interest is in you, which surely clarifies the position. He is charming her to get information. He will be doing well to get anything at all. Even I have not succeeded.'

They were back to battle with a roll of drums, Maggie noted, and her enjoyment drained away completely. She admitted that she had been thrilled at the idea of being alone with him, but all he was going to do was be stiffly silent. The need to shock him and score points overrode her caution.

'As I'm supposed to be helping you with Ana,' she said quietly, 'I should perhaps tell you that in my opinion Mitch is falling in love with her.'

'And kissing you?' The derisive query showed her that as a bombshell it had failed to explode. Maggie did that.

'A quick peck on the cheek is not kissing, *señor*!' she pointed out fiercely. 'I know that quite well now. Yesterday morning you explained it all to me.'

'Then perhaps you should pass on the lesson to Señor Mitchell,' he grated. 'Or is a chaste kiss on the cheek all you need from a man after all?'

'I need nothing from a man!" Maggie snapped, turning on him violently.

'*Pobrecita*,' he sneered. 'It is too late to save you.'

That ended any sort of conversation and Maggie sat fuming for the rest of the journey, very glad that Felipe sat as silently. They were right back where they had started.

Jaén, the centre of the largest olive-growing area of Spain, sat close to the Sierra Morena, the Dark Mountains. Felipe told Maggie this somewhat grudgingly as the city came in sight. It was one of the first cities conquered by the Arabs in Andalucía and it still retained a Moorish atmosphere. To Maggie, though, the city was dominated by the superb cathedral and the rocky slopes of the mountains.

As they drove through, she looked around with great interest but Felipe was still taciturn and moody. He glanced at his watch and deigned to speak again.

'We will have lunch at the Castillo de Santa Catalina,' he stated firmly, glancing at her as she tightened up. 'Do not be anxious, *señorita*. It is a *parador*, a hotel now, not the abode of one of my ancestors.'

'I never imagined it was,' Maggie bit out. She had, though, just for a minute. She had forgotten that many castles in Spain were now official hotels. All the same, most of them were splendid and she was glad she had put on a dress today.

It still looked very much like a castle, the interior with great arched ceilings, and Maggie was determined to enjoy everything and ignore the dark, brooding air of the man who kept her closely at his side. After lunch he took her to the shops in the wide, tree-lined avenues, and though from time to time she was out of his sight she had no doubt whatever that he still thought she would rush off to telegraph news to her magazine if she got half a chance. It was taking all the pleasure out of things and Maggie's lips drooped like a disappointed girl's.

'Come along,' he said quietly when she informed him solemnly that she had finished and stood with arms full of parcels. 'I noticed you admired the cathedral. I'll take you for a closer look.'

'It's quite all right,' Maggie said bleakly. 'I know you're wanting to get back to the hacienda.'

'I am not,' he sighed. 'Sometimes I feel that I am imprisoned there. Come along, Maggie. Give me a moment's peace.'

Of course it stunned her into silence and she never answered at all, not even when he reached out and collected most of her parcels, carrying them himself.

'Rather a lot of swimsuits,' he murmured wryly.

'I — I bought other things,' Maggie said quickly. 'I didn't know we would be in Spain for so long.'

'Will you really be expected back soon?' He walked along not looking at her, but there was a great deal of dark interest in his voice.

'There's no deadline, if that's what you mean,' she said gloomily. 'They're expecting results, though, and I haven't done a thing yet.'

'Why?' He looked at her then, his dark eyes intent.

'I don't know,' Maggie said fretfully. 'I suppose I'm too interested in Ana. She seems to be taking all my time. I find her so sweet and I can't bear it that she's blind. I'd do anything to get her to be able to see again.'

There was a catch in her voice and he took her arm as they came to the magnificent front of the cathedral.

'Let us sit here in the sunshine and contemplate the building,' he suggested softly. 'It is well worth looking at. It took over two hundred years to complete. Inside, though, it will be cool and dim; here there is life and the Plaza de Santa Maria is beautiful too. It is better to be in the sun.'

It was. They sat and looked at the wonderful façade of the cathedral and watched people walking by, and Maggie was glad to stay in the light. There seemed to be enough darkness without seeking more—Ana's blindness, Felipe's secret ways and her own.

'I got a present for Ana,' she said suddenly, shrugging off the foreboding that threatened to sweep over her. 'I'll show you,' she added, taking the wrappings off a long figurine.

It was a dancer, carved out of black wood, polished to brilliance. It had fine singing lines and Maggie ran her hand lovingly over it.

'She can't see it but she can touch it. It's lovely to touch.' She held it out to him and after one startled glance at her Felipe took the figure in his hand, running his fingers over it. The sight of his sensuous touch made Maggie's heart accelerate wildly and her cheeks flushed as he looked up at her.

'She will like it. I did not bring her anything; I spoil her enough as it is.' He handed the figure back and Maggie began to wrap it up rather frantically, worrying about her hot face. 'To touch is a pleasure but not necessarily a sin,' he added softly, seeing her confusion. He looked into her rather desperate eyes and Maggie ran the tip of her tongue anxiously over her lips. He stood abruptly, picking up the parcels and pulling her to her feet, his hand firmly on her arm, his face back to derision.

'At this point it would be wise to go,' he remarked drily. 'Some parts of the road back need steady hands.'

Maggie knew exactly what he was talking about. For a mad moment there she had wanted to lean towards him and feel again that hard mouth on hers. She had looked into the midnight-dark eyes and it hadn't seemed to matter at all that the plaza was a very busy place. Sensual pleasure had been swirling around her.

She never thought at all about the hacienda until they were almost back there. What she was thinking about was her own changed character. Felipe wasn't angry any more either. He had gone back to calling her Maggie.

'I'll give the carving to Ana after dinner, *señor*,' she said in a rush, trying to get her mind to other things and seeking strict convention like a suit of armour.

'That will be nice,' he murmured ironically. 'Do you think you could also play by your own rules and drop the formality? My name is Felipe.'

'But you're a count!'

'And it does not impress you at all,' he pointed out drily. 'As it has never impressed me either, you can pretend that I am normal and address me by my name. You may treat this as an order.'

'When I've thought about it,' Maggie mused, surprised at her own reluctance. 'It will take a while to get used to it.'

'It will not. You owe it to me. Last night I contained my irritation and said that odd word — Mitch.'

'You could call him Bruce.'

'It is just as odd. You may judge the state of my temper in future by the way I address him. I am not amused to see him so close to my sister.'

'But surely you know that he prefers me?' Maggie taunted, the devil getting into her, a peculiar excitement rising at this subtle duel.

'Perhaps that does not amuse me either,' he said quietly, slanting a dark glance at her. 'Do not make the mistake of teasing me, Maggie. The road is troublesome but there are places to stop.'

That silenced Maggie, of course, and his smile was all masculine satisfaction. The female had been put in her place, her legs made to tremble. The trouble was, Maggie's legs *were* trembling, and it certainly wasn't fear.

Felipe had gone before Maggie came down for breakfast the next day. She couldn't find Ana anywhere either. Things had gone well the night before. Ana had loved the carving and Maggie had not been able to wait until after dinner to give it to her. As Ana had run her hands over it, seeing with her fingertips, Felipe had watched Maggie until her face was flushed as a rose and her heart was beating madly. He had not needed to say anything. His amused thoughts hung in the air between them.

Ana had been full of her day, saying how Mitch had described England to her, explaining so openly how they had spent their time that Felipe relaxed and became quite gracious to Mitch.

Now, though, with breakfast over and no sign of Ana, Maggie began to search for her. Mitch did not know where she was either and seemed to think that she had been deliberately keeping out of his way. It was more than likely if Felipe had spoken to her, and as Mitch went off alone, looking very disgruntled, Maggie continued her search. She was beginning to understand Felipe's desire not to let Ana out of his sight — the same protective urge was in her too. Once beyond the perimeter walls of the hacienda there was wilderness and danger for a young girl who could not see.

Maggie had never been to the big barn before, the one that had looked so imposing from the air. It stood well away from the other buildings and this morning the great doors were partly open and she looked inside carefully.

What she saw astonished her because Ana was there and no mistaking it. The barn was as high and big as a huge hall, an earthen floor strewn with finely scattered straw. Light came from windows in the roof and Ana was bathed in the light, the barn dim around her. She was mounted on a white horse, her back straight, her head high, one hand gripping the reins and the other loosely at her side.

Felipe stood in front of her like a lion-tamer, a whip in his hand with the thong coiled out of the way, and for a second Maggie felt a wave of fear. He looked absolutely grim, advancing, tapping the whip lightly on the ground as the horse retreated rhythmically. It was like a dance without music, silence through the whole barn except for the tapping and the quiet thud of the hoofs.

'*Arriba*!' At the sudden order, Ana's hand tightened, the horse rose on its strong haunches, its forelegs pawing the air, holding an impossible stance at a dangerous angle. The whip stayed in front of it, daring it to descend, and Ana suddenly wheeled away impatiently.

'It is enough, Felipe! Soon my knees will bleed, if my hand does not drop off first.'

'It is not enough and you know it!' Felipe snapped. 'Schooling is not achieved by walking languorously around the property, listening to sweet words from the Englishman.'

Maggie saw Ana blush brightly and was surprised to hear her snap back.

'You are a slave-driver, Felipe, and you do not know what we talk about!'

'Training should take all your time! Do you wish to compete or do you not?' he grated, turning to keep his eyes on his sister as she circled him expertly.

'You know I do!'

'Then work!' He suddenly cracked the whip and the horse leapt astonishingly, all four feet off the ground in a strange little manoeuvre like a startled cat. Maggie gasped but Ana sat like a rod, a smug little smile on her face, only one hand still on the reins, no sign of panic. She landed expertly, her face filled with satisfaction and rebellion, and Felipe grinned, a sort of ferocious pleasure about him.

'You remember well, little one,' he growled in amusement. 'Anyone else would have been on their head. Pace him around once more and we will call it finished for today. This once I am prepared to give in.'

Ana cantered to the side and began a beautifully controlled walk to circle the barn, the horse stepping high and stately, back again to the beautiful dancing movement, and Maggie was so entranced that she never moved. It was as Ana approached the door that Maggie came into the line of Felipe's vision and the smile died on his face very speedily.

'What are you doing here?' He looked angry enough to whip her and Maggie had difficulty standing her ground. Obviously she had walked into some sort of a secret and Felipe was not at all amused by the fact.

'I came to find Ana,' she explained lamely.

'And stayed to pry?' He seemed to be towering over her before he even got near but Ana heard her voice and stopped, cantering back towards her.

'Maggie? You are there?'

'Of course she is here,' Felipe snapped. 'When is she not here? She is a journalist.'

'He is angry because I will not work all day,' Ana explained, sliding easily to the ground. 'He is not too happy either that I was ready for him when he cracked the whip. It is not schooling but a nasty little trick he has to get the better of me. He did not succeed. I hope you saw that, Maggie?'

Felipe was glaring at Maggie but she decided to ignore him.

'I saw it. It looked very dangerous to me—all of it.'

'I am well trained,' Ana laughed, showing a confidence that astounded Maggie. 'One day I will represent Spain. Felipe has promised.'

She almost danced away, out of the door and into the sunlight, blithely leaving her horse to her brother whether he had intended seeing to it or not. He glared at Maggie for a second longer and then gathered the reins and turned back to the door.

'I should have known,' he muttered. 'There are no secrets when Maggie Howard is on the job. Now you know a little more.'

'It would look wonderful in a photograph,' she remarked thoughtlessly, and was once again at the receiving end of annoyance.

'Keep him out of here!' he rasped. 'This place is out of bounds to both of you.'

'I'm supposed to be writing about the horses,' she pointed out firmly. 'I can't think of anything better than that to write about. It's the only exciting thing that's happened here.' It was deliberately provocative because she was disappointed that he was back to antagonism after yesterday, and he shot a startled glance at her before giving a low, dark laugh.

'Indeed? I will have to think up some excitement for you, *señorita*.'

They both knew what he was talking about but Maggie dropped that line of banter at once. She was not in his class as far as taunting came, and readily admitted it. She did not want to be dragged further into her growing feelings for him either.

'Why are you doing all this with Ana?' she asked seriously. 'Does she really want to compete?'

'Yes. At first I would not even consider it but it fills her days, or at least it did until you arrived with your *friend*. I was afraid for her, anxious all the time, but she is like a monkey when she is in the saddle. Nothing can dislodge her and she has the talent for it. If she never sees again,' he added fiercely, 'at least she will have this, something that few can do with brilliance. I will make her brilliant, or die in the attempt.'

'Does she want to be brilliant?' Maggie asked softly and he gave a strange laugh, leading the horse out into the sunlight and locking the door securely again.

'She does. It is a deep-seated desire that lingers from long ago. She wishes to be like me, another famous Santis. I would not pander to it but she must have *something* to make her life special.'

Once again he sounded full of pain and Maggie put her hand on the strong brown arm; she just couldn't help it. She was beginning to feel the pain he suffered.

'She is special,' she said softly. 'She's beautiful and courageous with a sweet nature and a very fine dignity.'

He stopped and looked down at her, his eyes moving over her face.

'And you wish to write about her.'

'It would add a great deal of colour to my article, please Mr Parnham and give Ana the right kind of Press coverage.'

She was almost holding her breath. He clearly despised her profession and wanted to protect Ana, but he was considering it. He continued to look at her, his eyes narrowed.

'It would depend upon whether I trust you or not,' he murmured. 'I will think about it.'

Maggie felt annoyed but she had more sense than to argue. She knew perfectly well he didn't trust her. He was all take and no give. He turned the horse away and walked off, ignoring her, and she went back to the house seething with annoyance. He usually left her feeling like that.

Maggie was by the pool, enjoying doing absolutely nothing and watching Ana swim when Mitch came up looking extremely displeased.

'Just what the hell are we doing here, Maggie?' he snapped. 'It's unbelievable. We came to do an article on this place and I doubt if you've written one word. I'm behaving like a tourist with an expensive camera. I can't think of one shot I've taken that would be out of place in a family album. I can see both of us getting the sack.'

'I know.' Maggie kept her eyes closed and felt incapable of worrying. 'The trouble is, we're both completely absorbed with Ana. I've got to admit that the magazine rarely enters my mind.'

'You can bet we've entered Richie's mind,' Mitch muttered. 'He's used to us going off for weeks and never getting in touch but he always has something to show for it at the end. This time we'll have nothing. He knows where we are, don't forget. If he decides to ring us we'll be short of a few answers.'

'I don't care. Do you know that?' Maggie announced, sitting up and looking at him seriously. 'I've run your warning past my mind and it's failed to register. The fact of the matter is, I'm interested in Ana. I'm almost desperate to help her. It's utterly frustrating because I know there's something else that would give me a clue. Nobody is about to tell me, though.'

'She's not likely to tell *me*,' Mitch stated grumpily. 'She's been keeping out of my way all morning.'

'Ah, well, she had something special to do this morning,' Maggie said in what she imagined was a soothing voice, well aware that once again she was keeping a secret from Mitch.

'What was it?' He turned on her eagerly and Maggie realised she had set herself an embarrassing trap and walked right into it.

'I can't tell you.'

'What is this—ostracise Mitchell day? What do you mean, you can't tell me? We're supposed to be a team.'

'Er—it's not my secret,' Maggie said evasively, getting up and wondering whether to dive into the water and refuse to surface.

Ana came out of the pool at that moment and it was a good job she couldn't see or her face would not have had the happy smile.

'Mitch?' She looked towards him and he frowned indignantly.

'Oh? You've decided to speak to me, have you?' Ana's face fell instantly at his tone and Maggie could have hit him. She didn't get the chance. Ana turned to leave, unhappy and going too fast. Her foot slipped on the smooth tiles and a frightened little cry left her lips about one second before Mitch moved like lightning and caught her, his arms tightly around her, holding her close.

Felipe strode round the corner at that precise moment and he simply exploded.

'Remove your hands from my sister!' His voice cracked out like the whip earlier as he surveyed the frozen tableau. Mitch, however, was in no mood to take orders and his voice was savage too.

'You wanted me to let her fall and injure herself? Maybe you should take better care of her. Or are you too busy taking care of Maggie?'

Maggie was stunned and Ana gave a bitter cry and pulled free, hurrying to the house and out of sight.

'Explain that very odd remark!' Felipe advanced dangerously and Maggie came to life, jumping between them.

'Stop this!' she ordered angrily. 'I'd like to point out that you've both upset Ana. She has enough problems without you two raging like mad bulls. She slipped and Mitch caught her,' she snapped at Felipe. 'That's what you saw. And as to you,' she continued, turning on Mitch, 'just what did you mean? Keep me out of your moronic speculations and don't snarl at Ana!'

'I'm not at all impressed, Maggie,' he rasped, filled with unusual rage. 'I've got eyes in my head and you're not at all daunting any more. The old Maggie has gone. Señor de Santis has softened you up.'

'Really?' Maggie raged. She took one step forward and toppled Mitch fully dressed in to the swimming-pool without a moment's hesitation. She was enraged and not at all pleased when Felipe threw his head back and roared with laughter. She stormed off and away and the last thing she saw was Felipe helping Mitch out of the pool, his dark face still lightened by a very wide grin.

The air was still singed with temper at lunchtime. Felipe had definitely stopped being amused and Ana had appeared merely because she considered it polite. That much was very evident to Maggie. The girl was subdued and unhappy and Maggie felt like attacking both Mitch and Felipe.

'I'm running out of film,' Mitch said stiffly when the uncomfortable meal was almost over. 'If I can borrow transport I'll go and get some.'

Ana excused herself quickly at the sound of his tight voice and as she left the room Felipe fixed Mitch with a sceptical eye.

'How strange you did not think of this yesterday,' he commented. 'You could have gone to Jaén. Am I to understand that this will be a continuous joint effort until one of you manages to send out news?'

'What news?' Mitch asked angrily, no sign of his quiet ways left. 'I've photographed everything in sight and nothing at all will appeal to the readers of *Query*, much less to the editor. Maggie has done absolutely nothing. If you think we've anything to send out then search for it. I'd be delighted if you found something. It may save my job.'

'I would have thought a photographer came prepared with much film,' Felipe grated, not all pleased to be spoken to like this.

'I don't normally waste shots on happy families,' Mitch assured him acidly, and Maggie stood and looked at them both wearily. Mitch, of course, was not now speaking to her.

'I think the time has come to call this assignment over,' she said quietly. 'It's quite true. I haven't done a thing. There's nothing to inspect and without my words the photographs are useless unless Mitch decided to sell them to the national Press. I can assure you, though,' she added for Felipe's benefit, 'we care too much about Ana for anything like that to happen.'

'What are you talking about?' Mitch asked angrily. 'Why should we even think such a thing?'

'Señor de Santis is afraid that publicity will bring reporters here, reporters of the unwanted variety.'

'Over my dead body!' Mitch stormed, so obviously annoyed that Maggie knew without any doubt that telling him to guard Ana with his life had been a superfluous order. He was angry enough to be violent in his defence of her, angry enough to be jealous when she kept out of his way.

'Well, I think we should go,' Maggie finished lamely, waiting for Felipe to show fury at Mitch's possessive attitude to his sister.

'No!' Both men said it together in the same explosive voice and Maggie wasn't sure which one to look at. Felipe won. Her eyes turned on him and he looked thoughtful.

'I apologise,' he said quietly, looking at Mitch. 'You have both helped Ana and I did not even have the right to ask. Jorge will take you for film,' he added. 'He knows the road and the city. It is time to go now if you intend to go today. Evening comes early and the road is not too good.'

'I may as well go now,' Mitch said ungraciously. 'Nothing else seems to be happening.' He walked out of the room as Felipe rang for Jorge, and Maggie made off too but didn't quite escape.

'So you were not merely teasing,' Felipe said quietly. 'You really were warning me. For some reason he is angered out of his normal self and clearly Ana is miserable. We have an extra problem, eh, Maggie?'

'I don't think you have,' she said with a cold look at him. 'You'll just issue further instructions. Mitch and I will get the order of the boot more than likely.'

'Unless you re-tell the story of Felipe de Santis and his blind sister as you write about the Hacienda de Nieve,' he pointed out stiffly, his warmth gone at the cold look on her face.

'It just wouldn't fit in under my byline,' she said acidly. 'You haven't shot anyone yet — no interest therefore to Maggie Howard's readers.' She walked out of the room with the dark eyes following her. The only thing she could do now was find Ana and mend a few fences. What the hell! She was going to tell the truth. The truth had never worried her before. If Felipe didn't like it he shouldn't have agreed to their coming and got them embroiled.

She tracked Ana to her room, a room further along

the balcony, and in her usual manner she came straight to the point.

'Don't sit up here miserably because two men are quarrelling over you,' she said briskly. 'The thing to do is exploit their weakness, not sink into gloom.'

'They are not fighting over me, Maggie,' Ana said unhappily. 'Felipe is just angry that Mitch touched me and that I did not repulse him quickly. Mitch was as usual just being kind. Anyway, he has not spoken to me all day.'

'Hmm!' Maggie said grimly. 'That's understandable if you're a man. Mitch is merely sulking. He thinks you were avoiding him. He didn't know why, so, like a man, he decided you didn't want to speak to him.'

'Oh!' Ana turned her lovely eyes towards Maggie. 'He cared that I was not — not available?'

'He certainly did,' Maggie assured her. 'He's going off to Jaén for film. Having used most of it up taking shots of you, he realises that when anything happens that he should cover he's going to look very foolish with no film in his great big camera.'

Ana's face lit up and they both heard Mitch going across the courtyard, talking to Jorge.

'He is there now?' Ana asked eagerly. 'What is he doing?'

'He's talking to Jorge and looking up towards your room,' Maggie said drily, wondering just what Felipe would use to kill her if he found out about this piece of sabotage.

Ana stood up and waved, smiling down, and then turned to Maggie.

'He saw me?' He had. He hesitated and looked as if he was going to abandon the trip, his smile coming back with such speed that Maggie stood too.

'He saw you. On your way, Señor Mitchell,' she called down. 'Come back in a better frame of mind.'

She got the old lop-sided grin and sank back to her seat, pleased with a daring deed well done. Well, Mitch was her friend again and Ana was happy. Aunty Maggie to the rescue. Ana sat too, her face glowing.

'Do I look all right, Maggie?' she asked shyly. 'Am I really beautiful?'

'As beautiful as an angel,' Maggie assured her. 'Forget the seeing, go with the feeling, but don't tell your big brother.'

Big brother was not too pleased at dinnertime. He had just taken a call when Maggie arrived to eat.

'The car has broken down,' he told her, looking suspicious. 'They cannot get it repaired until morning.'

'Not guilty,' Maggie said firmly. 'I never touched it. Don't worry, he's not about to escape with film concealed about his person. The used film is probably in his room, and in any case, he develops his own.'

'I did not imagine he was about to escape,' Felipe said coolly. 'I saw his departure and heard your advice. There is nothing wrong with my hearing, Señorita Howard.'

'Eavesdropping is despicable, Señor de Santis,' she said, her cheeks beginning to glow.

'So is treachery,' he countered softly.

'Treachery is one of those funny things,' Maggie informed him sarcastically. 'It all depends whose side you're on. Now me, I'm firmly on Ana's side,' she finished as Ana walked into the room with a smile on her face.

She was to prove that sooner than she expected.

# CHAPTER SEVEN

SOMETHING woke her in the night. Maggie had no idea what it was and no notion of the time but as she opened her eyes every sense was alert. She had lived many times on the edge of danger and she knew better than to sink back to sleep. The courtyard was no longer floodlit but the moon was brilliant, filling the room with light, and Maggie slid from her bed and went quickly to the long window that led to the veranda.

She almost cried out in shock as she saw Ana moving quickly across the old court, drifting like someone in a dream. She was moving to the great gates and before Maggie could react the white-gowned figure had gone around the corner and out of sight.

No thought was necessary. Maggie acted, racing from her room and running to the stairs, not waiting to put on slippers or a robe. She knew without being told that Ana was walking in her sleep and she was filled with horror at the girl walking through the gate and beyond, perhaps waking late and not knowing where she was, unable to see. That alone would be terrible without any danger she might encounter on the way.

She was through the door and out into the courtyard within seconds but Ana had already gone and all Maggie could do was follow. She did not call out. She had some idea that you should never wake a sleep-walker. She had to get her before she went through the gates and she was thankful for the bright moonlight.

Ana was going down the stony path, almost at the gates. She seemed to be almost floating and Maggie was astounded that the sharp stones had not given her enough pain to waken her. Maggie's feet seemed to be on fire with each stone she encountered. She grimaced

113

at the pain and, putting on a spurt, she took a careful hold of Ana's arm and stopped her.

Ana just drifted to a halt, turning without demur as Maggie moved her to face the house. She went back as she had come, fast asleep and docile, her face expressionless. It was uncanny and Maggie was never so glad to see the light from her own room and get Ana back indoors. So far not a word had been spoken and if she could manage it the girl would not even know tomorrow.

It all proved to be very easy. She moved to Ana's room and got the girl on to the bed, lifting her legs and preparing to cover her. Then she remembered the stones. She risked putting the lamp on and was pleased to see that Ana's feet did not look as bad as her own felt. Maybe there had been a bit of floating going on there after all? Maggie found Ana's bathroom and was just coming back in with a towel she had partly wet when Felipe appeared in the doorway.

She silenced him before he could speak, shaking her head and putting her finger before her lips. Then she bathed Ana's feet as best she could. She was just drying them when Ana stirred and opened her eyes.

'Maggie? Why are you here? Is it morning?'

'No. You were having a bad dream. I heard you. Let's get you covered now and back off to sleep. How did you know it was me?'

'Your perfume. It is nice. I would like you to leave the light on.' Maggie's heart leapt at the request. Could Ana see? Was her sight returning after all?

'How do you know it's on now?' she asked carefully, and Ana turned over comfortably, smiling to herself.

'Because if it were not on you would not be able to see.' She snuggled under the sheets and Maggie made a wry face, her hopes dying.

'Think you're clever, don't you?' she teased, stifling her bitter disappointment. Ana gave a small, gurgling laugh and Maggie leaned forward and kissed her cheek.

She just couldn't help it. 'Back to sleep, smarty,' she said softly.

Ana seemed to fall asleep at once and Maggie went out, closing the door quietly.

'What was all that about?' Felipe followed her to her room, his dark eyes intrigued. He was still dressed and Maggie looked at her watch. It was just on midnight. She sat abruptly on the bed, suddenly feeling the strain of the rather alarming excursion into the night.

'Ana was walking in her sleep,' she explained wearily. 'I just happened to wake up and see her in the courtyard. There was no time to get you because she was making for the gate.' She rubbed her hands on her cheeks, surprised to feel quite shaken. She had been in some tight spots with her work but this had hit her hard because she cared very much about the girl. 'I was scared she would get out and off the estate, wake up and — and. . .'

'She has never done this before,' Felipe said worriedly, pacing to the long window and back. 'I must make sure it cannot happen again. That being the case it will be necessary to tell her tomorrow. I have to fix some sort of bolt on her door that she cannot reach.'

'It's going to make her feel trapped,' Maggie protested. She shuddered. 'I keep thinking she might have gone out on to the balcony instead.'

'Do not tear yourself apart with worries of that nature,' he advised quietly, coming to stand over her and look down at her seriously. 'Surely a person walking while asleep will imitate normal events?' He suddenly looked down at her feet. 'Why were you bathing Ana's feet?'

'Oh, she was walking over the stones and I wondered if she was cut, but she wasn't. It was just a precaution.'

'And you? Did you not also walk over the same stones?' he asked softly. 'You ran after her without even stopping to put on slippers. Let me see your feet.'

'No!' Maggie came to flustered life. She had been so

worried that she had not given one thought to the fact that she was here in her nightdress with Felipe standing looking down at her. Now she was very much aware of it. 'I — I'm fine.'

'I think not,' he insisted. 'You were limping as you came across Ana's room and I would think you probably came off worst in this adventure.'

He had her foot in his hand before she could stop him and his indrawn breath made her aware that it looked as bad as it felt. He let her go and straightened up.

'Do not move,' he ordered. 'Not one step. I have a first-aid kit in my bathroom.'

'I can go to my own bathroom and see to things myself,' Maggie said with an anxious look at him.

'And bleed all over my carpet, *señorita*?' he enquired tauntingly. 'You will stay right there.'

He was back in a very short while and to her embarrassment he knelt and bathed her feet carefully, putting a plaster on a slight cut after he had dried them. Maggie felt like curling up and crawling away. It was not just the fact that this imperious man was doing this for her. It was also the terrible pleasure it gave her when he touched her. There was nothing at all in his touch but kindness and efficiency but she had to bite into her lip to stifle the urge to stroke the dark head that bent close to her and his hands on her skin sent melting sensations through her that utterly drowned out any slight pain from the sharp stones.

'There.' He stood and picked up the small bowl he had brought, walking through to her bathroom to empty it. His eyes were intently on her as he came back and he put the things he had brought on her dressing-table, ready to remove. She wished she had not put the lamp on in the first place because she was sure he would be able to fathom out how she felt. Those dark eyes had a way of burning into her.

He walked and pulled her to her feet.

'Now you will take the advice you gave to Ana. Back to sleep, Maggie.'

'Suppose she walks out again tonight?' Maggie asked anxiously, looking up at him.

'For tonight I will put a chair by her door, out in the passage where she will bump into it. I doubt very much if she will venture forth again, however.'

'Maybe not,' Maggie murmured worriedly, biting into her lip again as he continued to look down at her.

'It is a long time since anyone cared for you as tonight you cared for Ana, is it not?' he asked softly, his hand coming to tilt her downcast face. 'And yet there must have been some man who wished to. You have hidden for a long time, Maggie, and missed so much.'

'I've lived as I wanted to live,' she assured him breathlessly, unable to look away now that his eyes had captured hers. She was very much aware of her state of dress and warmth seemed to be flooding through her.

'But now you are not the same.' His arm came round her, very intimate through the thin material of her nightdress. It seemed to send sparks right through her. 'You have stepped from the barrier you had built and in spite of your flashes of temper you are softly feminine and vulnerable.'

'I'm not.' She tried to shake off the feelings but it was sheer impossibility and he smiled down at her.

'Oh, Maggie. Stop fighting.'

His dark head bent, his lips trailing over her face gently, and Maggie swayed forward, immediately entranced, immediately hungry for more, turning her head to meet the lips that captured hers. His arms tightened round her then and he pulled her against him, accepting the soft body that wanted to press against his own.

'There is something about you that arouses every instinct in a man,' he murmured, looking down into her face. 'I do not think you even realise the danger you walk towards so willingly.'

She did not. The old Maggie had known how to defend herself, how to keep anyone at arm's length, but this new person delighted when Felipe touched her, glowed with languorous warmth and melted instantly. She was melting now and his hands tightened.

'You cannot be so innocent,' he said tightly, but even so his teeth nibbled at the lobe of her ear as his breath quickened. His hand slid to her breast and he turned impatiently back to her lips as he felt the surging, swollen arousal.

Maggie moaned ecstatically as his thumb teased the tight, dark nipple that pressed sharply against the thin skin and her arms slid around his neck, her fingers lacing in his black hair as she kissed him back wildly.

'*Por Dios!*' He suddenly swung her up into his arms, looking down at her with burning eyes. 'If you cannot protect yourself then I must protect you. You risk yourself for my sister, ignore your job and your orders and collapse into my arms. You know how to make a man hungry, Maggie Howard, and I am really beginning to believe that you are not aware at all of the consequences.'

He put her into bed and drew the sheets over her and Maggie came back to the reality of the lamplit room with a bang as he strode away, collecting his tools of mercy and making for the door without looking at her.

'I—I'm sorry,' she managed, her voice trembling.

'A few moments more and you would have been,' he assured her drily. 'Maybe very soon you will need a chair at your door too, *señorita*. It will need to be inside, though, and tightly under the handle.' He walked out, closing the door firmly, and Maggie quickly switched off the lamp, huddling down in bed and waiting for her heart to right itself.

She could not believe the way she had behaved with Felipe, and she didn't blame him at all. She was well aware that she purred inside like a cat if he even looked at her and the whole thing filled her with amazement.

Maybe there was something wrong with her? Maybe she had been locked in her self-imposed prison for so long that now she was unable to control herself at all.

It seemed unlikely. She had no urge whatever to throw herself at Mitch. At least the idea restored her humour. Mitch would probably have a fainting fit. Felipe did not show any sign of anxiety. He simply swept her into his arms and held her. She was still tingling with pleasure and her cheeks burned when she realised that if he came back he could just take up where he had left off and she would not do a thing to stop him.

Felipe was still having breakfast when Maggie went down the next morning, and it caught her off guard. Normally he had already gone out to the horses but now she had to face him and she was feeling quite unsure of herself.

'You are no worse for your midnight adventure?' he asked quietly as he helped her to her seat.

'No. I'd almost forgotten.'

The defensive remark had him slanting a rather grim glance at her and she felt even worse.

'I — I'm sorry about. . . I was upset and. . .'

'I did not help matters,' he acknowledged tightly, his hands cradling his coffee. 'You are getting close to Ana and seem to have taken quite a responsibility on your shoulders. I have no right to ask it. Perhaps you should go back to England and forget all about us.'

Maggie was horrified at the wave of dismay that came from nowhere. He wanted her to go, and she felt afraid as she realised that she did not want to go at all. She had let her guard down to an enormous extent and the idea of going back to her old life was actually frightening. She felt absurdly safe here with Felipe de Santis, grieved that he wanted to get rid of her.

'If you want us to go. . .'

'I did not say that!' he rasped suddenly, glaring at her. 'What I want is not and never has been important.

You have been pressurised into coming here and I have added to that by demanding your help. Twice you have placed yourself at risk for Ana. She is my responsibility and I am merely suggesting that you may want to go home. I will not oppose it. You may leave Devlin Parnham to me.'

Maggie looked down at her meal, feeling thoroughly miserable.

'I don't want to leave Ana,' she confessed quietly and he had no time to do anything other than look at her intently because Ana walked in at that moment, looking bright and determined.

'When Señor Mitchell gets back I would like us all to have a nice little trip,' she announced, sitting and smiling round almost as if she could see them. It was as well that she couldn't, Maggie thought, because Felipe looked almost thunderous.

'Perhaps our guests would not like a trip,' he reminded her stiffly.

'Well, they have been cooped up here for some time,' Ana pointed out. 'An excursion would be fun and Mitch could take a lot of good photographs.'

'You seem to have it planned,' Felipe noted drily. 'What trip do you have in mind?'

'We'll go to Granada,' Ana announced firmly. 'Mitch will like it.'

'And what about Señorita Howard?' Felipe wanted to know. He did not look at Maggie and she noted only too well his return to formality.

'But she is a writer and Granada is wonderful. You would like to go, Maggie?'

'Er—yes. I'd like it very much,' Maggie managed and Felipe shot her a look of disbelief. He imagined she was merely indulging Ana.

'When do we go?' he asked in a taunting voice, once again prepared to indulge his sister.

'Today,' she said determinedly. 'As soon as Mitch

returns. We can stay all night. You can book our hotel, Felipe.'

He said nothing but Maggie saw the black brows rise in mockery and she reassessed her conclusions. He was not merely indulging Ana. He was letting her lead for reasons of his own. That had to be suspicious, and as she went into the hall later to go to her room he followed.

'So, you would like to go to Granada?' he taunted. 'You are quite prepared to let Ana lead you onwards?'

'She's leading you too,' Maggie reminded him quietly and his hand came as it often did to tilt her chin imperiously.

'You believe so? Maybe I am letting you get a step closer to civilisation, *señorita*. A night in a good hotel with many nationalities around you may bring you to your senses and perhaps you will not wish to return to the Hacienda de Nieve.'

'I'm in complete control of my senses!' Maggie snapped. 'Ana is quite right, anyway. I can get some notes for my article in Granada and Mitch can get some shots. Afterwards, I'll come back to collect my things and go. Ana has probably told me all she is going to tell me.'

It alerted him at once and he took a tight grip on her arm as she swung away to leave him.

'What has she told you?' he grated.

'Enough for me to know that she was very unhappy just before your father died. Enough for me to know that this house was not a good place to be when he was alive, not good for either of you. Ana was trapped here, though, by the sound of it. She was seventeen and not exactly in charge of her own life.'

'So you *do* blame me for her blindness,' he said menacingly. 'I can well imagine that you do not wish to leave here until you have proof. What a good article that will make for *Query* and Maggie Howard!'

He spun round and walked off and Maggie looked after him in dismay. She hadn't meant anything of the sort. It was his guilt speaking, the burden on his conscience. It was quite impossible. Why couldn't he just talk about it reasonably? Nobody would ever get close to a man like Felipe de Santis and she refused to acknowledge that she wanted to get close.

Mitch came back and Maggie did not see how Ana greeted him, but it was plain that he was restored to his old self, cheerful and easygoing. He was pleased about the trip and it was clear that Ana had planned it for him and for her own secret reasons.

Maggie was not cheerful as they set off for Granada. Felipe was grimly silent, obviously still annoyed. When he came to the car, Ana had established herself in the back with Mitch and he would have needed to be extremely unpleasant to order them out. He did not, but it added to his anger and Maggie was pleased that she had not been there early. He would certainly have blamed her.

'Perhaps this trip is a good idea after all,' he rasped quietly as they came to the car almost together. 'She is in his presence far too much.'

'He seems to care about her and, like it or not, Ana cares about him too,' Maggie said miserably.

'Merely because he is the only man around and she has become used to him,' Felipe grated. 'He is not of our world and she will finally realise it.'

'Yes, I can see that,' Maggie said caustically, inexplicably hurt. 'Proximity. Things do tend to get out of proportion when you're shut up in the mountains. I suppose once we're back home this will look like a dream to both of us, rather unlikely in the face of reality. An amusing little interlude.'

He had not one doubt about what she meant and that was the end of any sort of conversation. Felipe was able to sit with a perfectly thunderous face knowing that his sister could not see it.

He had timed their arrival for early evening with few

people around. It was an overcast day and not the height of the season as far as tourism was concerned. On the way he maintained his cold silence and they were both aware of Ana and Mitch who talked endlessly. From time to time Maggie saw Felipe glance at them through the rear-view mirror. Mitch would be dispatched speedily as soon as they got back and so would she.

They saw Granada before they got there and Maggie's heartbeats quickened. This was a first for her too in more ways than one. She had never been to this exalted place before and it seemed to be a place of dreams. The city rose at the edge of a green plain, nestling in the foothills of the Sierra Nevada, and as Mitch gasped Ana realised they had arrived.

'Please stop, Felipe,' she begged. 'If it can be seen from here then let Mitch look and take photographs. Maggie will want to look too.'

Maggie did want to look and Felipe reluctantly stopped the car so that they could get out. Mitch instantly walked off with Ana, describing what he saw, his camera working, and Felipe stood stiffly beside Maggie, his face tight.

Granada glowed in the golden evening like a jewel suspended between the snowy Sierra Nevada and the rich green of orange groves. The Alhambra palace glowed too, red in the evening sun, and Maggie was entranced.

'Thank you so much for bringing us,' she said softly. Her soft words did not get a soft reply.

'It is the last place I would have chosen to bring my sister,' he grated.

'But why? She wanted to come.'

'For Señor Mitchell, not for herself. A strategy to have him with her for longer and to please him.'

'Perhaps she just wanted to come here,' Maggie protested.

'You do not think that, *señorita*. Look at it, the golden

evening, the snowy mountains, the citadel of the
Alhambra. Do you imagine she does not wish to see it
again herself? One could spend a lifetime in Granada
and still not see everything. Ana can see nothing. I will
quote you from long ago if you doubt it: "Life holds no
greater sadness than to be blind in Granada." That she
would come here, knowing that she would see nothing,
makes me realise how infatuated she is with him.'

Maggie was silent and he suddenly took her arm.

'Oh, come along! It is not your fault. You are merely
a woman who pretends to be fierce and, after all, you
have been manoeuvred by men in spite of your supposed
ability to take on all comers. I have ordered you about,
Devlin has ordered you about and even Ana has dragged
you here to please a man.'

'I wanted to come,' Maggie muttered, quite agreeing
with him that she had come off worst in everything.

'Did you?' He looked down at her sardonically. 'Then
let us continue and make the most of it. It is too late
tonight to begin exploring. Tomorrow we will walk you
off your feet.' He led her to the car, helped her in and
started the engine. It brought the other two back
smartly and Maggie knew that Ana was enjoying herself
no matter what Felipe thought. She was here with
Mitch and to a woman that was more exciting than any
worldly beauty. Maggie sat silently, shocked that she
should have thought such a thing. She was glad to be
with Felipe even when he was raging.

'The Alhambra Palace is the eighth wonder of the
world and it is the only remaining medieval Arab palace
anywhere in the world. The Moors wept at leaving
Granada and still mourn its loss in their evening pray-
ers. It is a place of air and water, colour and light.'
Ana's sweet, clear voice gurgled with laughter. 'I know
this because I have been here several times when I was
younger. The guide was most boring but I remembered
the poetic bits.'

Maggie glanced at Felipe and she was pleased to see

him suddenly smile to himself. His dark eyes glittered across at her, catching her wide-eyed and anxious appraisal.

'So far she does not seem to know how sad it all is,' he murmured. 'Perhaps we should cheer up too, *paloma*.' His eyes lingered on her clear grey gaze and Maggie blushed hopelessly, but all the same she was suddenly happy.

The hotel overlooked the Alhambra. Coming through the crowded, often narrow streets had been tricky and Maggie was pleased to find that the hotel was modern and luxurious.

'I have ordered rooms facing the mountains,' Felipe informed them. 'There is a moon tonight and you will be able to see the glacier from your balcony.'

'I'll get a few shots,' Mitch said eagerly, but Felipe did not even glance at him.

'I had thought that perhaps Señorita Howard would be able to gaze and dream,' he murmured, his sardonic gaze on Maggie. 'That is what writers do, is it not?'

'Not writers like Maggie,' Mitch said emphatically. 'She's hard-hitting, not dreamy.'

'Perhaps I am wrong about you,' Felipe said softly as they went to the lift. 'But I think he does not know you as well as I do.'

'I've known him a long time,' Maggie said desperately, knowing quite well that she was being taunted and feeling just a little defenceless. 'I work with him. I've worked with him in lots of hard places.'

'Perhaps. But then you were hard too. Spain has changed you. It changes most people. Behind those eyes I see a romantic mind.'

'You'd better not believe it!' Maggie snapped, stung into action.

'That sounds like a threat,' he murmured. 'A dove cannot threaten. I feel quite safe.' All Maggie could do was glare and he simply smiled derisively.

She was glad to dive into her own room and as he

had promised her little balcony faced the Sierra Nevada.
Already the sun was glowing red, its rose-tinted light
catching the glitter of ice. It was quite, quite beautiful
and Maggie shook her head in exasperation. Felipe
knew her better than she knew herself, it seemed. She
was becoming utterly dreamy in this land.

When they went into the crowded dining-room for
dinner two people sprang up and came straight towards
them. One was a very beautiful blonde and the man
with her was tall and fair too, almost as fair as Mitch.
She soon found that they were English and she also felt
a certain amount of unexpected dismay because the
woman flung her arms around Felipe and kissed him.

Maggie expected him to look annoyed but he did
nothing of the sort. He looked very pleased with himself
and introduced them to Maggie and Mitch.

'Friends from England,' he said quietly. 'Peter and
Candace Rainford.' Maggie found herself being inspected
closely by two pairs of eyes and Candace Rainford's
green eyes hardened as she looked at Maggie's face and
the shining mahogany-red of her hair. She ran her gaze
over Maggie's dress and her lips tightened.

'I think my wife is too busy admiring you to speak,'
Peter Rainford said. It might equally hold for him too.
He still let his eyes run over her and Maggie was both
embarrassed and shocked at the look in them. Neither
of them had even acknowledged Mitch.

'You know, I'm getting quite used to this invisible
business,' Mitch muttered to Maggie when they were at
last settled to their table. 'It's funny, everybody could
see me before I came to Spain.'

She knew what he meant. Even now the two
Rainfords were watching from their own table and
Maggie's face flooded with colour at the looks she was
getting from Peter Rainford. His wife never noticed. Her
attention was solely taken up with Maggie and Felipe.
It squashed all thoughts of enjoying this trip.

They were squashed even further when the other two

joined them for coffee and later in the bar. Peter Rainford was unpleasantly attentive but his wife was quite happy with Felipe, and Maggie's heart sank as they arranged to go round the Alhambra with them the next day. All she wanted to do now was get out of here because it was pretty obvious that this woman had known Felipe when he was enjoying himself on the coast and there was definitely something between them. Perhaps the Rainfords had one of those marriages where each did his and her own thing? It made her thoroughly miserable.

She was even more miserable later because almost as soon as she arrived in her room she started to have toothache. It wasn't really very bad but it was a dull ache that made her realise she would never get to sleep. As there was hardly ever anything wrong with her, Maggie did not carry any sort of pain-killer, but she needed one now. She rang the desk and was told quite coolly that there was no such thing in the hotel. They also pointed out that there was no room service and Maggie sank back down to sit on the bed and nurse her aching face.

She couldn't sit there for long. She began to pace about and finally went out on to the balcony to watch the mountains and try to take her mind off a pain that she was sure would keep her awake all night. It was dark now, the sky a velvet-soft black, but as she watched the moon came out and changed the colour of the sky, caught the glitter of ice and dimmed the stars.

Maggie could not enjoy it, though. She was too busy holding her aching face and she gave a soft murmur of pain as she drew her dressing-gown closely around her.

'*Qué pasa?*'

She looked up sharply and saw Felipe standing on his balcony next door, half hidden by shadows. She was so stunned to find him close that she never answered.

'Answer me, Maggie! What is wrong?' He came

forward until he was bathed in moonlight and Maggie found her voice somewhat belatedly.

'Oh, it's nothing. I've got a bit of toothache.'

To her astonishment he came to the edge of the balcony and simply climbed across, ignoring the drop.

'You'll fall!' She gasped out the words but he took no notice whatever and landed lightly beside her.

'I did not. All I did was arrive more quickly than going round to your door.'

'Well, thank you but there's nothing you can do.'

'I can find you a dentist even at this late hour.'

'I don't need one. It can wait until I get back to London,' Maggie said quickly. She didn't want to go to a dentist; even her own dentist scared her, and it couldn't be much — her teeth were perfect. 'All I wanted was a pain-killer but they said at the desk that there were none in the hotel. Anyway,' she added with a rueful look, 'I couldn't even get a cup of tea. They said there was no room service.'

'Did they?' Felipe breathed and strode across to the phone. She couldn't follow the swift flow of Spanish but she could hear the reply.

'*Sí, el conde! Ahora mismo!*'

Whatever they had been ordered to do they were about to do it right away and Felipe replaced the phone with a dark frown on his face.

'Give them five minutes,' he said grimly. 'They have to get the tablets too.'

'They'll not arrive in five minutes,' Maggie calculated, hugging her face.

'If they do not, then I will arrive at the reception desk,' he stated flatly, and she revised her opinion.

Just over five minutes later she had taken the tablet and Felipe was pouring her a cup of tea, and Maggie looked at him in amusement.

'I suppose I could have got action like that if I'd been a count,' she mused.

'I did not announce my title.'

'But they know you.'

He shrugged and looked at her wickedly.

'They also know now that I am in your room, *señorita*. The call came from here and the waiter saw me.'

'I'm not bothered,' Maggie informed him pertly. 'If you hadn't come I would have been up all night.'

'So I have my uses?' He leaned against the dressing-table and showed no sign of leaving, and Maggie looked away, her quick rise of spirit fading. 'I am becoming accustomed to watching over you,' he added softly. 'Now that you have discarded your masculine disguise you seem to need a good deal of attention.'

'I can easily go back to normal,' Maggie got out quickly but he reached out and captured her hand, spinning her towards him and catching her in his arms.

'Can you? I doubt it.' He ran his hand gently over her cheek. 'How do you feel now? Is the tooth better?' She knew he was speaking to her as if she were either an idiot or a child but the momentary fight had quite gone and she just nodded, looking up at him.

When she just kept on looking at him he threaded his hands in her hair and let it drift through his fingers, watching the deep red glow in the lights. His eyes met hers, dark and secret with a light behind them that she could not fail to see.

'You want me to stay, don't you?' he asked quietly and Maggie shook her head. It was the only way she could lie to him. It brought a smile to his face because he recognised the lie though no word had been spoken and he trailed his lips across her burning cheek before catching her mouth lightly with his own.

She made no move to resist, she never could and he lifted his head, looking down at her in amusement, putting her carefully from him and turning to the door.

'As you seem to panic when I am in any danger,' he murmured sardonically, 'I will leave by the normal method. In any case,' he added, turning to look at her intently, 'the fact that I was in your room at this hour will be all over the hotel by morning.'

'It won't!' Maggie gasped anxiously.

'It will. In Spain we like a good gossip. All the waiters will be envying me tomorrow.' Maggie looked outraged and his eyes glittered with laughter as he left. She pulled herself together and went to bed. He was merely taunting in his usual manner and she was quite pleased with herself that she had managed to retain some control when he'd kissed her.

The memory of Candace Rainford had helped there, and she had to admit it. Well, Felipe couldn't go to that woman anyhow because she was with her husband no matter what signals she had been giving Felipe. The thought of the husband had Maggie getting out of bed and locking her door securely. The fact that Felipe could climb over the balcony didn't bother her at all because she knew he wouldn't, in spite of his words.

# CHAPTER EIGHT

THE visit to the Alhambra next day was not the joy
Maggie had hoped it would be, at least not initially,
because Candace and Peter Rainford were there at
breakfast and even more resolute in their determination
to join Felipe's party. Ana was not pleased.

'Why can't they do something else?' she muttered
angrily, her arm sliding into Maggie's as they left the
hotel. 'I don't find them at all pleasant. When they are
in Spain they visit the hacienda. Felipe knew them ages
ago and they just keep coming. I wanted this to be just
the four of us. After all, *I* planned it!'

'Perhaps they'll go?' Maggie whispered hopefully.

'You had better not believe it!' Ana informed her
gloomily. 'That woman dotes on Felipe—but do not
mention it to him,' she added hastily. 'He would not be
pleased. She is married, you see.'

Maggie did see, and she also saw the way Candace
clung to Felipe's arm, laughing and talking as if her
husband did not exist. Felipe didn't seem to mind and
Maggie remembered his life on the coast, wealth and
beautiful women. This woman was certainly beautiful
and all the pleasure went out of the morning.

In spite of that, when they arrived, the place took
hold of her. So early, there were few people about, and
she had the chance to feel the ambience of the last
Moorish palace. The Moors had ruled Granada for over
seven hundred years and this was their monument, the
gardens where nightingales still sang and the beauty of
the Alhambra—'the red castle'.

Maggie stayed with Mitch and Ana. She helped
Mitch to describe the coloured tiles and gold mosaics,
the arches and alcoves. They watched her remembering

things she had seen before. It seemed to Maggie that the whole place was almost hanging in the air because it seemed impossible that such slender columns could hold such intricate, lacy arches and ornate ceilings. Everywhere there was the murmur of water and finally Ana said rather sadly, '*Por favor*, just let me listen.'

Maggie remembered Felipe's words and understood his reluctance to come here with his sister. Ana seemed to find pleasure in simply listening, though. There was the Court of the Myrtles with its pool and lovely arches, the Court of the Lions with fountains of twelve carved lions and over a hundred slender pillars. She looked down and saw Ana's hand firmly held by Mitch and a twinge of sadness fluttered over her as she wandered away. She would never have thought that she could feel like this in her whole life. She wanted Felipe to be there to enjoy it with her.

Her imagination ran riot, peopling the place with great caliphs, beautiful ladies in gossamer veils and fierce soldiers to guard the purple-red ramparts. It was part of the deep past of this country, a past that could always be felt.

'So here you are, alone as usual.' Maggie actually jumped as Felipe suddenly appeared and she looked round hastily for his clinging companion and her rather bold husband. They were nowhere to be seen.

'I just wandered off,' she said lamely, feeling still upset and slightly anxious.

'I am beginning to think that, with you, wandering off is not advisable. You get into trouble. Come with me.' He took her arm and Maggie protested.

'What about your guests?'

'They are not my guests.' He stopped and looked down at her. 'You are my guest and I am attempting to be nice to you. Are we to fight about it?'

'No.' Maggie looked at him in a bemused way and he smiled to himself, leading her onwards.

'Where are we going?' Maggie asked worriedly.

'This room, the Hall of Secrets. Come, I will show you something. I expect it still works.' He led her inside and left her at one side of the room, walking softly away and stopping to face her at the other side. He was smiling at her mystified look and suddenly he whispered, 'Maggie.'

It was the merest whisper but she heard it clearly, her grey eyes opening wide.

'Oh! How did you do that?'

'It is the acoustics. This is called the Hall of Secrets but it is the wrong place to whisper them. Every sound can be heard in any part of the room.'

He was only whispering then but Maggie heard clearly and her face lit up with delight.

'Do you have any secrets, *paloma*?' he whispered, his eyes intently on her entranced face.

'None that I'd tell you,' she said clearly, and he laughed, coming back to collect her.

'Let us get out of here before you deafen me,' he suggested.

Whether by accident or design, they managed to go around without seeing any of the others and Maggie allowed herself to be selfish. She knew that Ana was safe with Mitch and the last person she wanted to see was Candace Rainford.

They walked in the beautiful gardens of the Generalife and seemed to have the place almost to themselves, and Maggie turned to Felipe as they stood and listened to the running water.

'Oh, it's so beautiful. I must come here again one day.'

'Perhaps you will come here often,' he said softly, smiling down at her. 'You are at home in this land, Maggie. Is that not so?'

It was, but she wasn't about to admit it.

'I can't afford to be.'

'But why?' His hand captured her face and turned

her towards him in the old domineering manner but his eyes were not at all hard. 'We have not quarrelled once.'

'That's true.' She suddenly smiled up at him. 'It must be the atmosphere.'

'We have created our own,' he said softly. 'There was no one to interfere.'

Interference came at dinner that night. The Rainfords joined them and Maggie supposed that Felipe could not very well say no. All the same, her dreamy enjoyment faded and as Felipe was almost smothered by Candace and Mitch was utterly involved with Ana, who refused to be more than primly polite to the new arrivals, Maggie found herself encumbered with Peter Rainford, who sat as close as he could get and set out to entertain her. It was something she could have done without and finally she was struck with inspiration.

'Please excuse me,' she murmured, glancing round. 'I really must go to my room. I have a toothache.'

She was gone before they could utter a sound and arrived at her own room grinning widely, pleased with herself and only a little upset that Felipe was with that woman. Maybe he couldn't get away and, after all, he had been wonderful to her earlier.

She was somewhat startled to find a waiter knocking on her door very soon and he came in bearing a tray of tea and a pain-killer, looking at her sadly and murmuring his regrets. It took a minute to dawn and then she had great difficulty in not laughing. She had even fooled Felipe. He had sent assistance with the same speed as last night.

Maggie was thankfully drinking the tea, the pain-killer still on the tray, when Felipe arrived, knocking on the door and striding in when she opened it.

'How are you?' He looked at her sympathetically and she had to get her face in order quickly.

'Er — I'm all right, thank you.' She looked just too guilty for words and knew it, and Felipe's dark eyes flashed to the tray and the still unused tablet. His eyes narrowed as he looked back at her.

'You recovered without it?'

'Well, I. . .' Maggie tried to think fast but failed, so she lifted her head and looked at him defiantly. 'I didn't have toothache. I just wanted to get out of there.'

She could see it was the wrong thing to say and his black brows rose coldly.

'I expect my guests to be polite, *señorita*,' he informed her icily.

'Then point that out to Peter Rainford, *señor*!' she countered, glaring at him. 'I don't expect to have to eat my meal with someone breathing down my neck.'

'I assumed you were enjoying it, *señorita*.'

'No,' Maggie said sweetly. 'The enjoyment was all yours. *I* don't encourage anyone who is married.'

'And you assume that I do,' he stated angrily. 'Next time you are in distress I will know to leave you to it. I do not allow a woman to make a fool of me!'

'One was certainly trying hard,' Maggie murmured, swinging away from him.

When he pulled her back she expected very harsh reprisals but all she got was a very speculating look.

'Jealous?'

'Of course not!' She struggled to get away but he pulled her towards him, laughing down at her.

'Then do not sound so jealous, *señorita*.' Just as she thought he was going to kiss her he let her go and strode to the door. 'Do not throw the tablet away,' he warned sardonically. 'Wickedness brings its own punishment. Yours may well be toothache.'

Maggie sat on the bed and fumed but it was not long before she started to smile. He had acted quickly to help her. She lay in bed and thought about it. Nobody had looked after her for years, he had been quite right about that. It was warm and soothing to think that Felipe cared if she was in pain. She went to sleep with a smile on her face, pushing the thought of Candace right out of her mind.

All she could see was Felipe's face, his dark eyes, the laughter that had been so ready this morning. He was quite right. She was happy in Spain. Her old character seemed to have gone far away and here she didn't need it back.

There was no laughter on Felipe's face next morning. The luggage had been collected and Maggie went down to the foyer, ready to leave. Felipe was there alone and his face tightened as Mitch and Ana came in together. Maggie followed his irritated gaze. They were making very little forward progress. They were laughing and talking as if nobody were there at all but the two of them and she could see the source of Felipe's annoyance. They were holding hands.

Maggie went across to him quickly, trying hard to think of something to take his mind off his sister's minor crime, but she hadn't much chance of that.

'Very soon she will have to face the fact that Señor Mitchell will leave.'

His voice was icy and Maggie sighed. They were back to square one.

'You can't keep her forever,' she pointed out quietly. 'One day, some man will come along. Even if you send Mitch away and forbid her to be with him, it's going to happen one day.'

'I am aware of that,' he informed her coldly. 'I do not jealously guard her. Give some thought, though, to the fact that she may not recover. She is young, beautiful, she touches the heart—even yours. Should I let this develop until she wishes to leave Spain and go with Mitchell? Should I see my sister alone in a foreign country—blind? How long will he care for her? How long will he take on the responsibility of a wife who is blind and helpless? Perhaps one day he will turn to a woman who can see, live the life he wants, share things.

We are two different cultures. We have lived different lives.'

'Perhaps love conquers everything,' Maggie said quietly, feeling his pain as she always seemed to do.

'Do you have experience of it?'

'No. Never in my life.'

'Then you can hardly expect me to take the chance. I will not allow Ana to take the chance either. One day she may be left alone and weeping in a cold grey city with people who do not care.'

Maggie did not answer because it was true. Hadn't she been there herself long ago? And she had not been blind either.

'You have no comment to make, *señorita*? No ideas?'

'No,' she said bitterly. 'I think I've run out of both ideas and time. At the end of the week we'll go home. If Mr Parnham doesn't like it and we're both fired then I don't much care. As I told you when we first met, I have a reputation, we'll survive.'

'So you are hard as ever underneath it all?' he said derisively. 'Spain has not really changed you.'

'That was never the point of the exercise, was it?' she asked quietly. 'You invited me into your life of your own free will. I've tried to help you with Ana but I never intended to change. We all have to survive. I survive as I am. As you say, I live in a cold grey city where few people care.'

She walked off outside and stood by herself, taking one last look at the Alhambra. She was still there when Ana joined her. Mitch was also looking at the Alhambra and taking a few more shots.

'Are we ready?' Maggie asked Ana, but the girl slid her arm into Maggie's and shook her head.

'We were, but now Felipe has been captured by the Rainford woman. She will keep him talking even though he is angry.'

'What is he angry about?'

Maggie tried to sound quite innocent but Ana smiled a touch bitterly.

'Oh, Maggie! I know when he is angry. I do not have to be able to see his face. He is always angry now.'

'That's because he argues with me,' Maggie pointed out, but Ana shook her head again.

'No. Since you came here he has laughed more and been amused more than he has been for the past two years. Do not expect him to always be amused, though; he is a very powerful man. Even so, I know you please him, Maggie. His anger is with me.'

'I think only because of Mitch,' Maggie said hastily but Ana disagreed.

'That perhaps is making things worse, but Felipe has been angry with me since my father died. He blames me. I can hear it in his voice. I try to pretend it is not happening but I know it is.'

'Ana! I'm sure you're wrong.' Maggie felt the girl's misery and tried to stop her but Ana had said all she was about to say. Mitch came back to them and that was the end of the conversation.

So that was always in Ana's mind? Not enough surely to make her blind? Maggie was puzzling over it as Felipe came out and normally she would have told him at once, but he was not alone. Candace Rainford was clinging to his arm and he did not look as if he minded in the slightest. Her husband fastened his eyes on Maggie and that was enough to have her going after Ana and Mitch very quickly, her temper bubbling. If Felipe thought she would take the husband off his hands while he amused himself with Candace he was very much mistaken! When he came to the car and waved goodbye to his odd friends, Maggie sat unsmiling. As Ana was doing the same, both Mitch and Felipe looked less than happy. It was a shame about Mitch, but as to Felipe, it served him right!

* * *

Richie caught up with them the next morning. She was called to the phone just before breakfast and she knew who it was before she even heard that deep Australian twang.

'Mitch is ordered back home,' he informed her at once.

'You mean we have to come now, right away?' Her heart sank. She just did not want to leave here. Ana was telling her things bit by bit and in any case, annoyed or not, she didn't want to leave Felipe. He meant too much to her. With Felipe she didn't feel alone.

'Mitch comes back, not you. Old Parnham phoned about ten minutes ago. He wants you to stay as long as you think necessary. I know you're up to something, Maggie. It's damned annoying that you and Parnham have this arrangement. I don't even know what it is and I'm the editor.'

Maggie didn't even answer that one.

'Mitch isn't going to like this order. Do you want to tell him yourself?'

'I don't!' he snapped. 'You're the big boss. I've never known you back off from anything or anybody. You're doing something I don't know about. You can damned well tell him yourself!'

He rang off and Maggie looked ruefully at the phone. She wasn't the big boss here. She seemed to be nothing but a woman here. Mitch was going to fly into a rage.

She told him during breakfast. It was no use putting it off and she was sure that Ana should know at the same time. It had to be faced.

'I've just had Richie on the phone this morning,' she announced quietly. 'He's caught up with us.'

'And?' Mitch turned to look at her steadily and she did not miss the quick glance that Felipe cast in her direction.

'I've got two weeks' grace—at the moment,' she told Mitch quietly. 'You fly back to London tomorrow. Richie has something he wants you to do.'

She was aware that she was making it up as she went

along but she certainly didn't want to repeat what Richie had actually said.

'I'm not going!' Mitch glared at her as if she had ordered him back all by herself. 'We work together. Why single me out?'

'I expect it's because I'm writing and it takes longer,' Maggie confessed with a shrug. 'You haven't an excuse in sight, Mitch. You have to go.'

He looked explosive and to Maggie's surprise Felipe intervened. All of them had seen Ana's face. She was taking it badly, closing up like a flower that felt the sun going down.

'Don't be too hasty,' Felipe advised quietly. 'I can fly you out of here tomorrow morning. Think very carefully today and talk it over with Maggie. You need further photographs, I imagine. Come with Ana and me this morning and watch her school her horse. If you need shots of Ana de Santis, get something worthwhile to show your readers.'

It had the effect of startling all of them and silencing any other refusals. It silenced Maggie most of all because she had assumed that Felipe guarded this secret and she had never mentioned it to Mitch. Ana went off to change, looking very downcast, and Mitch went to collect his camera. It left Maggie facing Felipe and she looked straight at him.

'Why?' No other words were needed and he stood, walking to the window and looking out at the courtyard that was bathed in sunlight.

'I cannot forbid you to write about us,' he acknowledged. 'You must have something to show for all your time here. It was Ana who drew you here and even though Devlin is behind all this they will expect an article.'

'I can just write about the hacienda, the mountains, Granada,' Maggie pointed out.

'No.' He turned and looked at her. 'I have thought

about it. If anyone has to tell the story of Ana de Santis I want it to be you.'

'Why are you changing your mind?' Maggie asked quietly.

'Something you said. Publicity for Ana's riding. You care for her. You will do it best. You will do it carefully?' he added, his tone sounding suddenly a little dangerous, and Maggie stopped as she reached the door.

'You can judge for yourself,' she reminded him, her clear eyes on his frowning face. 'You've demanded to see everything we do before we go.'

'You are submitting to male domination?' he asked drily.

'I seem to have little choice as far as you're concerned.'

For a second he looked at her intently and then walked over to stand and search her face with dark eyes.

'I do not wish to see either the photographs or the article,' he said quietly. 'I trust you. I know you care about Ana. Write as you think fit.'

'Thank you.' Maggie felt her heartbeats quicken as he continued to look down at her.

'I would like to know every secret in your head,' he murmured quietly.

'No hope of that. I — I go in two weeks.'

'And will you be happy to go?'

'If I've done what I set out to do,' Maggie managed defensively. She went quickly through the door and out of his sight, racing up to her room to recover. Would she be happy to go? Oh, no! The more she saw of Felipe, the more she wanted to be near him. It was quite mad. He recognised how she felt and did nothing to encourage it. One day soon she would see him for the last time.

Ana and Mitch went riding after lunch. With the advent of Mitch's immediate departure, Felipe had softened somewhat, but Maggie noticed that one of the men rode

discreetly behind them. Ana was no doubt used to
having a chaperon as she was blind, and in this case it
was the only way they would be allowed to leave the
proximity of the hacienda. Decorum demanded it in any
case.

Maggie watched them go and then went to find
Felipe. She had not told him what Ana had said to her
and it was time that he knew. At first she couldn't find
him anywhere but finally she tracked him down to the
big barn. This time it was not Ana who took her breath
away. Felipe did that in a much more devastating way.

When she peered cautiously round the door, remembering his annoyance at her earlier prying into this
place, she literally froze to the spot. It was not because
she feared drawing his attention to her presence. It was
because not for anything in the world would she have
disturbed him and missed this spectacle. So many
feelings raced through her as she stood there — admiration, delight and pleasure that almost brought tears to
her eyes.

He was on a white horse but even she could see that
it was not Ana's horse. There was something about it
that made it different and she did not know if it was a
horse in a class of its own or if that was the rider. He
was sitting straight-backed, Spanish-style on a Spanish
saddle that looked expensive and richly trimmed. There
were heavy Moorish stirrups and over his trousers he
had chaps of dark, soft leather, the glitter of silver down
the sides.

Memory came from deep inside her and she stood
entranced, feeling the same romantic dreaminess she
had felt as a girl. He held her attention as nothing else
ever had and she knew without memory that this was a
master, a genius at work. In the quiet of the huge place
the horse performed like a champion and Felipe looked
like another person from the man she now knew.

He was old Spain, aristocratic and severe, a tremendous hauteur about his face. When the horse reared as

Ana's had done it seemed to grow in stature, holding the stance endlessly and then leaping into that strange jump, its forelegs not touching the ground. This time, though, it was not once as Ana had managed it. This time the horse repeated the process and Maggie was spellbound.

It was urged into the air again, kicking out with its back legs, seeming to hang there motionless, and then on hind legs it walked several steps forwards. There was not a sound except the stamping hoofs and as she watched he allowed it to come to the ground, pacing it in that superb prancing way, its silken tail swaying.

The horse paced, high-stepping, wheeled and returned, wheeled again and Maggie watched, awe-struck, her reasons for being here initially completely forgotten. Finally she began to applaud quite spontaneously, her clapping sharp and enthusiastic in the silent barn where the dust rose in the shafts of sunlight.

He spun round in surprise and then he set the horse towards her, pacing slowly, strongly and rather menacingly. She didn't know if he was annoyed but nothing could wipe the admiration from Maggie's face.

'Felipe de Santis of Spain!' she announced clearly. 'Felipe the Magnificent!'

He just came on in the same purposeful manner and Maggie backed away, a little alarmed and suddenly remembering why she was here. From his expression there was not much chance of speaking to him at all and she cast a wary look behind her to the door.

'I need to talk to you.' She looked up into the haughty face but he said nothing at all. He merely continued to advance. 'I want to tell you something,' she added firmly. He just ignored her and Maggie felt the quiverings of alarm grow and turned to leave. The closer he got, the bigger the horse looked. As she turned he set the horse against her quickly, its strong shoulder nudging her away in another direction. It was impossible to escape. The horse was made to foil her every move, leaping forward as she moved quickly and turning her away. Finally she was backed into a corner by the door, the horse guarding any escape route and the man looking down at her with dark, fathomless eyes. So far he hadn't said a word but he spoke then.

'Before your arrival in Spain I had privacy. Now you seem to be in every place at once. You think I will forgive you everything?'

'You invited me to Spain. And as to this present situation one of us is going to tire eventually,' Maggie pointed out tartly with more bravery than she really felt. 'If you're going to be annoying I'll just stay here.'

'*Muy bien.* We will both stay.' His tone changed like magic and he dismounted with such easy speed that Maggie panicked.

'I'll talk to you at the house!' She raced from the barn and fled towards the house with a very red face, especially as she heard his amused and taunting laughter. She wasn't sure how annoyed he had been just then. You never could tell with him.

She was in the pool when Felipe caught up with her. She had been to her room and put on one of the swimsuits she had bought. It was a bikini, flower-printed and attractive against her dark red hair. The pool seemed to be a good place to stay. She had got herself all hot and bothered and she felt much safer in the water than she had in the barn. There had been a very masculine intention to punish in those dark eyes and she had a good idea what the punishment would have been. She would be keeping a tight hold on her feelings from now on.

Soon, like Mitch, she would have to go. It filled her with sadness but she was a realist. This was just a very brief interlude in her life. She didn't know whether to be grateful or alarmed that her time here had softened her. There was still a world to face and in that world she had learned to take care of herself. There would be no Felipe to spring to her aid when she had an accident or a toothache.

He had looked after her since she had come here. Maybe he was like that with every woman, Spanish chivalry. He was certainly nice to Candace Rainford. That thought merely deepened her gloom and she floated on the water, wishing that Ana would come back. Anything to take her mind off Felipe.

She was at the deep end of the pool when Felipe suddenly surfaced beside her. She had never seen him come and she regarded him worriedly.

'You don't duck people under water, do you?' she asked, backing off.

'Not if they panic about it.' He could see the beginnings of fear at the back of her eyes and he kept quite still. 'I considered it, but then, you take care of my sister and applaud my skills. It would be ungracious.'

She was still wary and he moved well away from her.

'Swim to more shallow water,' he said quietly. 'I want to know why you came to look for me.'

After one more anxious glance she took off for the other end of the pool and a quick look showed that he was already on his way, moving with powerful strokes and keeping well clear of her. He hadn't seemed very pleased and he was waiting when she arrived.

'I am ready,' he announced, pulling himself to the edge of the pool and looking down at her with no expression on his face to give her any clue about his attitude.

'I learned something from Ana when we were leaving Granada,' she began, looking up with what she hoped was an intelligent determination to talk.

'You have waited a long time to tell me. Perhaps I had better hear it now.'

Maggie noted his rather irritated expression and wished she had told him straight away. But how could she have? That Rainford woman had been there. The thought made her frown, especially as she admitted that the feeling when she remembered was jealousy.

'Ana thinks you're angry with her.'

His black brows rose sceptically at this small amount of information.

'She is not far wrong at the moment. She neglects everything for Mitchell. This is not really an outstanding piece of detective work, *señorita*.'

Back to formality, he watched her wryly and Maggie slowly began to boil. Did he call that woman *señora*? Of course not. This was just for her, and all she was doing was trying to help.

'It has nothing to do with Mitch,' she told him flatly. 'According to Ana, this anger has lasted for two years. She believes you are more pleasant now than you have been since your father died, in fact.'

'*What?*'

She had his complete attention now and nothing about him was sceptical.

'I'm merely repeating Ana's words.' Maggie felt she had the upper hand to some extent and this had to be talked out. 'Look,' she said seriously, determinedly ignoring the sleek brown body resting beside the pool, 'you have to give some consideration to just about everything she says. There's some underlying cause for this blindness.'

'You imagine she is blind because she feels I am annoyed?' he rasped, looking at her as if she were stupid.

'Of course not!' Maggie snapped. 'She wouldn't feel like that unless something was troubling her, but neither of us knows what it is. Just think about it. She's going to be even more upset when Mitch goes and we've got to be ready for it.'

His eyes narrowed alarmingly.

'If this is some trick to manoeuvre me into allowing anything to develop there. . .' he threatened.

'It's developed already,' Maggie said angrily. 'I can

see how well you trust me too. I don't know why I'm bothering about trying to help. Don't alarm yourself, Señor de Santis. Mitch and I know our place. We know we're many steps down the social scale from the Santis family. What *you* don't seem to know is that I'm working for *Query* and not for you. I might just as well pack up and go if you can't even listen to things reasonably!'

She turned away impatiently, determined to swim off and leave him to it, but he slid into the water beside her and grasped her wet arm.

'I know you,' he said arrogantly. 'You could not simply go and leave Ana.'

'I could.' She glared up at him. 'I'm not at all surprised by your attitude. I think we might say that I know you too. Let me tell you, though, that it's years since I was ordered about; they dare not even do that in the office. Here, it's do this, *señorita*, do that, *señorita*, as if I'm a half-witted adolescent with nothing else to do with my time. I could be chasing some exciting story now!' she raged.

His dark brows rose in astonishment at this attack and then he slid his arms round her and pulled her towards him, looking down at her with the sort of expression a grown-up reserved for a naughty child.

'Behave yourself,' he murmured sardonically. 'You are frightening me with this temper of yours.'

'You're an absolutely impossible man!' Maggie snapped, struggling to get free, and he pulled her even closer.

'I know,' he murmured, suddenly smiling and bending his head to run his lips over her neck. 'I will always be impossible. If you know me then you know that too.'

Maggie put her hands up to push him away but as soon as they touched his skin her palms seemed to take on a life of their own, moving over the strong muscles, her fingers wanting to curl in the crisp black hair that lightly covered his chest.

'Maggie!' His voice was sharply warning but it was

not much use. She looked up at him with wide grey
eyes, her lips parted softly, and he tightened her to him,
his hand gripping the long, wet hair darkened further
by the water. 'Do you know how you are looking at me?'
he asked fiercely, but as she only shook her head he
tilted her face and searched frustratedly for her mouth,
crushing her against him.

# CHAPTER NINE

THERE was very little between them and Maggie melted at once, her legs against his as Felipe's lips moved over hers and his hands began to search her skin demandingly. Her breasts were tight and painful, crushed to his chest, and he pushed her back to the side of the pool, his weight pressing against her.

Maggie's hands clung to his shoulders, her lips fused with his, and when his knee nudged her legs apart in an impatient and very male act of domination she wound her leg around his calf without even knowing it. Her body softly accepted the hard evidence of his arousal and he buried his lips against her neck, his hand cupping her closer until it was almost like possession.

'*Dios*! Why do you do this?' he muttered thickly against her skin. 'You are like a cat, waiting to be petted, wanting my hands on you. You have even forgotten where we are. What if I take you? Will you then wake from this peculiar dream you have discovered and die of shock?'

His teeth bit into her shoulder but she only came closer and he made a low, frustrated sound deep in his throat, tilting her face and staring at her with eyes filled with burning darkness.

'Let me tell you something about men, Maggie Howard,' he grated unevenly. 'You have lived so long in your fortress that you have forgotten, even if you ever knew. A man will go so far and then he will snap. I have reached that point right now. You have two choices— flee from me or belong to me.'

She just looked up at him with bewildered eyes and he put her firmly away, turning to launch himself into the water.

'Then I will make the choice,' he rasped. 'Keep away from me. You are no longer safe.' He struck out in a powerful crawl and Maggie finally climbed shakily from the pool. She was trembling all over, embarrassed and ashamed, unable to believe she had behaved like that. His words were ringing in her ears now although they had had little impact before.

She had never responded to any man in her whole life as she did to Felipe. It was something she could not understand, something she never intended to do. It just happened. He was filling all her thoughts every minute of the day.

He was right. She was not safe here, not safe anywhere near him, and she should be thankful for his code of honour. She came to a very sad decision. She would have to leave. Whatever happened to Ana she would have to go back to England and stay there. She wasn't even capable of making cold decisions any more.

Mitch was deeply in conversation with Ana when Maggie walked into the dining-room that night. Felipe came in just behind her and Maggie spun round while there was just a moment of privacy.

'I've decided to go back to England,' she said quietly, not able to look at him. 'I'll go when Mitch leaves tomorrow. I can't help Ana except by being a friend and that's not enough. Mitch is too involved with Ana, as you pointed out. It's best if we both go at once. I can come up with some story.'

She walked off before he could answer and stayed very close to the other two until dinner was actually served. There was a great deal of gloom around the table. Ana was close to tears and Mitch looked utterly miserable. Maggie was numb with misery herself and Felipe hardly said anything at all. Each time she looked up his eyes met hers and she was unable to put a good face on things. Her ability to be cold and untouchable seemed to have gone as if it had never been.

She had found a man who meant more to her than

anything in the world and he was of another world, as he had told her. All that had happened was that her safe shell was broken and if it ever healed it would be filled inside with sadness.

Maggie was glad to go to her room. She got ready for bed and then stood on the balcony looking at the moonlit night and the mountains. It would have been better if she had never come here to Spain. She had been safe in her shell, secure from the world. Now she was only safe with Felipe because she did not fool herself one bit. He had changed her and changing back would not be easy. It might well be impossible.

He just walked into her room, closed the door and came across to her, and Maggie stared at him wildly as he took her arm, drew her from the balcony and shut the french window,

'I do not want you to go! Why are you doing this?' he asked savagely, spinning her to face him and gripping her arms tightly.

'I—I told you. I can't do anything else for Ana and my story will be easy to write with all the ideas I've got and——'

'You are going because you want me!' he snapped, giving her a shake.

'I'm not! I don't! It was just madness...'

'Then let us initiate some more of it.'

He pulled her into his arms, sliding his fingers into her hair and tilting her face. Before she could even breathe his lips were on hers, fiercely and demandingly in a kiss that seemed to last forever.

'Oh!' When he lifted his head and looked down at her, Maggie made a small inarticulate sound and his expression softened.

'*Te quiero*, Maggie. *Te quiero también.*'

'No! Be careful! I understand Spanish.' Unthinking, she put her fingers to his mouth and he caught her hand, kissing it urgently.

'I know. You have given yourself away many times. Why was I not to know?'

'It was my advantage. I wanted to creep up on you.'

He suddenly laughed and began to kiss her again, quick, hot kisses rained on her skin, her face cupped in his hands.

'You did not creep up on me at all. You exploded into my existence. You are impossible to ignore, Maggie.'

'It doesn't matter,' she sighed. 'I must go. I'm no help to Ana really. I should stick to what I do best.' She was giving no sign that she wanted to move. His lips trailing over her face were the greatest comfort she could think of. All her grief began to go and her eyes closed slowly.

'Stick to what you do best, then, Maggie,' he whispered. 'Kiss me.'

He pulled her close, folding her in his arms, but she buried her head against his shoulder even though her arms wrapped around his waist.

'You told me to keep away from you,' she murmured shakily. 'You said I would be safer.'

'Do you want to be safe?' He looked down at her and she couldn't look away from the dark, burning eyes. She shook her head slowly, her eyes closing again as he bent towards her and covered her lips with his own. She didn't want to be safe, not if it meant being away from Felipe. Every time he touched her she wanted more and more. He had shattered her barrier of ice but he had left her defenceless.

She melted against him and this time he simply gathered her closer. Hunger surged between them like fire and Felipe's body began to move restlessly, seeking her softness, his hand beginning to mould her closer still.

'Do you want comfort, or do you want me?' He lifted her face, looking down at her, and Maggie's slender arms tightened around his neck.

'You,' she whispered. 'Just you.'

'You speak without thought. You are back in that cloud of desire. Tomorrow will come, Maggie,' he murmured against her skin.

'I don't care!'

'But I care.' He lifted his head and looked into her eyes. 'I must care. You are not quite in this world at the moment. Tomorrow I would be consumed with guilt.'

'For no reason,' she said tremulously. 'You — you're the only person who — who. . .'

'Why?' He looked down at her, his breathing still uneven, and Maggie flushed deeply.

'I don't know. Maybe it's me.'

'Maybe it's both of us,' he said softly. 'Get into bed now and try to sleep.' He helped her into bed and stood looking down at her.

'I wanted you to stay with me,' she whispered with her usual honesty, and he sat beside her, his hand trailing over her face.

'And I wanted to stay. We both have a lot of thinking to do, I most of all.' He smiled wryly. 'I hope you know how much self-discipline I have just summoned up. Your mixture of innocence and desire is too much to keep refusing. I may never have the strength again.'

'What about Ana? She's unhappy.' Maggie came out of her trance, flushing rose-pink, her eyes avoiding his.

'Tomorrow. Everything waits until tomorrow. But tomorrow you do not go. I want you to stay. I will not fly you out of here, even if it means keeping Mitchell.' He tilted her face, looking at her deeply for a moment and then letting her go. He put out the lights and quietly left the room and Maggie lay in the darkness until the moonlight flooded each dark corner. Inside she was calm, a different calm. He was as perfect to her now as he had been when she had seen him as a child. Now she knew why it had to be Felipe.

In the heat of the moment he had wanted her but it had meant nothing after all. He was simply persuading her to stay, and she knew it. They were worlds apart and she would go finally, but there was a peculiar happiness inside her, not one drop of hatred left. Felipe was healing her somehow and all she had to do now was solve the mystery of Ana. If she could do that she would have done something for Felipe.

She got her opportunity next day. Felipe flew Mitch to the airport in the afternoon and there was thunder in the air in more ways than one. The sky was dark and threatening and Felipe had looked like that as he'd left the house. The smiling, persuasive man of the night before was gone.

Ana had wept bitterly and Mitch had stated quite categorically that he would be back. This alone had been enough to bring frowns to Felipe's dark face, but as they were leaving Ana's tears had suddenly been too much for Mitch to bear. He had pulled her into his arms, kissing her gently, and she had wrapped her arms around his neck.

Felipe could do nothing at all. He had started to move forward but Maggie had fixed him with her clear grey eyes and he knew what she knew herself—break into this now and Ana would refuse to stay here. She would go with Mitch. When everything was set down clearly, Mitch was the only one who could calm her.

'I'll be back,' he said urgently. 'I'm just going on another job for a while but I'll be back. Believe that, Ana.'

'I—I believe it. I shall wait each day.'

She had gone up to her room now as if she was simply going to sit there and wait for as long as it took, and when the plane disappeared from sight Maggie went to find her.

'Will he come back?' Ana knew it was Maggie as soon as she walked into the room. She was sitting on the veranda, her ears still straining for a sound of the departing plane.

'Yes. He'll come back.' Maggie sat down beside her. 'I know him very well and he means it.'

'Felipe will not let him.' Ana sat with bowed head and spoke in a forlorn voice. 'What can I expect? It is my punishment.'

'Felipe loves you! He won't attempt to punish you. You've done nothing wrong.' Maggie tried to sound firm. She knew how Felipe felt about Ana's future but this was not the time to point it out.

'I was not speaking of Felipe. He does not need to punish me—fate will do that. Felipe knows, though; that is why he is angry with me.'

'Look, Ana,' Maggie said sharply, 'this is nonsense. Felipe is not angry with you. He's just worried about losing you when you're not able to see. He doesn't know Mitch well enough to trust him to look after you.'

'It's more than that!' Ana spun round, her face pale. 'Felipe knows I killed my father!'

'Stop that!' Maggie said angrily. She could hear hysteria mounting and once again Felipe was not there. She always seemed to need him when she was on her own. 'Your father died of a heart attack. Felipe knows that. Everybody knows that.'

'But I caused it,' Ana whispered. 'I made it happen. Felipe does not know that. He merely suspects.'

She burst into tears and Maggie went to her, gathering her close. What a burden this girl carried. What had she allowed herself to believe? Was this the cause of her blindness?

'Hush.' Maggie rocked her in her arms and spoke softly. 'Tell me about it. It will help.'

For a long time, Ana said nothing, and Maggie was just beginning to believe that she would stay silent when it all came pouring out.

'I was home from school. It was the last time I would have to go. Felipe was away and the house was silent. I wanted to go to my friend's on the coast and then to join Felipe. It could all have been arranged by telephone. I was seventeen and able to look after myself. I was not even wanting to be alone. My friend's mother had rung to invite me and Felipe would bring me back. It was only normal but my father would not hear of it.

'For the first time I refused to do as I was told. He was very angry. He shouted and raged and Felipe was not there to help me. I just ran out of the room and went to pack some clothes. When he was not looking I came down and took the car. Felipe had let me drive around the hacienda but I had never been on a road.' She shivered and clung to Maggie, burying her head like a child.

'My father saw me going and it frightened me. I dared not think how he would be if I went back then so I had to go on. I had an accident quite close to the gates and Jorge came to get me and helped me back. I had banged my head badly and it was bleeding but my father was more angry than I had ever seen him. Maria came to help me but he sent her out. He was shouting again and then I fainted. When I came round my head was very bad and the first thing I saw was my father. He was lying close by and he did not move. When I came round again, I could not see and Jorge told me my father was dead.'

Maggie rocked her closer still. She could understand the guilt that Ana carried. She prayed that Felipe would hurry back because he was the only one who could convince Ana that she was not to blame.

'He had a bad heart, Ana,' she said softly. 'Surely Felipe argued with him too at times?'

'But not like me,' Ana wept. 'Felipe simply smiled and went his own way. And Felipe's arguments were logical, final. When Felipe was grown up my father was wary and kept his temper. I raged at him and screamed.'

'You were a girl and lonely.'

'There is no excuse. I was to blame.'

Nothing would move her from the belief and Maggie finally persuaded her to get undressed and have a sleep.

She sat with her until the exhaustion of grief finally drove Ana to sleep and silence, then Maggie went to wait for Felipe.

Now she knew, so easily, so quickly. Mental torment, a blow to the head and guilt. It was enough, or so it seemed to Maggie. Ana was hiding behind blindness, a cover for her guilt. It was a safe place to hide but she could not hide from herself and her imagination had made condemnation out of any unthinking word that Felipe uttered. Her imagined crime was something she could not tell her beloved and admired brother, and without that there had been nobody at all.

She was still pacing in the *sala* when Felipe came back. It was late, much later than she had imagined, and the storm was now beginning in earnest. It crashed around the mountain walls as if it would split them in two and she never heard the plane arrive. Felipe just walked in and she reacted as she felt — very relieved.

'Oh! I was worried about the storm.' The lashing rain had just started and as she spoke a great roll of thunder seemed to shake the house.

'You are afraid of storms?'

'No. They're fun. It was just that you were flying and. . .'

'I was flying into it. It did not quite get here in time. A little longer and I would have had some difficulty.' He poured himself a drink and then sat and looked at her. 'You were waiting for me?'

'Yes. I've been waiting for ages.' She looked at him a bit anxiously, wondering how she was going to tell him, and suddenly the hard face softened and he held out his hand.

'Come and sit beside me, Maggie. It has been a tiresome day. Whatever you want to say, say it. Only one thing could make me angry and that is if you demand to leave here.'

'It's not that.' She came to stand close and he took her hand, pulling her down to the settee with him.

'Then I can breathe easily.' He looked down at her and smiled. 'What is it? You are looking uneasy so it must be important to you.'

'It is.' Maggie chewed at her lip, wondering how to put it to him, but after all there was no way but straight out. 'I think I know why Ana is blind.' She could not have had more instant attention than she got then. He put his drink down and turned her to face him, his eyes intent on her face.

'It is because of me?' He looked devastated and Maggie instinctively touched his hard face, wanting to comfort him.

'No, Felipe, of course not. I never for one moment imagined that, no matter what you thought.'

'Then tell me.' He caught her hand and held it fast, his fingers tightening as she hesitated. 'Maggie!'

'She blames herself for your father's death. She thinks you suspect her and it seems to me that everything adds up to a good cause for her condition.'

Maggie quietly told him all that Ana had said and he heard her through in silence. He said nothing when she had finished. He just stared into space, his face tight with emotion.

'My poor Ana,' he said softly. 'For two years she has carried this burden. Without you I would never have found out.' He turned to her and took her face in his hands. 'Now tell me how to deal with it.'

'How can I tell you? I might be wrong. It seems to me that everything is balanced on a knife-edge.'

'You've solved every problem,' he assured her deeply, looking into her eyes. 'Whatever you say, Maggie.'

'She's asleep. Go and wake her and tell her you know. Explain it to her. Make her understand that there's nothing to feel guilty about.'

A slight sound at the door broke their rapt attention with each other and they both turned to see Ana standing there. She was in her dressing-gown, slight and pale, looking so forlorn that Maggie's heart lurched; she shot a quick look at Felipe and it said everything. How much had Ana heard?

'I'm not asleep,' Ana whispered. 'The storm woke me.' She just stood there and then her lip trembled. 'Maggie! You told him!'

The trembling accusation had Maggie looking forlorn too but Felipe took control immediately, standing and walking to his sister.

'Yes. She told me. Two years of misery, *querida*, because you would not tell me yourself. How long did you intend to suffer so needlessly? Would this have gone on forever if a grey-eyed *inglésa* had not stormed into our lives?'

'How could I tell you, Felipe?' Ana whispered. 'How could I tell you that I made Father die?'

'You did not. It was merely a matter of time and I knew it. It made me control my own rage, but, like you, I kept the information to myself.' He put his arm around her and led her into the room, and Maggie got up to go.

'Stay, Maggie,' Felipe ordered softly, but she shook her head.

'No. It's up to you. I don't belong here now. This is family.'

He started to speak but Jorge came in and asked about dinner and Maggie slipped out. She had done all she could do, found the truth. The rest was up to Felipe and any doctor he called in to help. It was a weight off her mind but her heart felt the weight now. There was no further reason to stay. She would never see Felipe again.

It was much later when he came. He knocked softly on her door and his face was still drawn when she opened it.

'How is she?' Maggie asked anxiously as he walked in.

'Coming to terms with the truth, I hope.' He sighed wearily. 'She has had a tray sent up to her and is now asleep. I have explained everything to her, told her it could have happened at any time. My father was his own worst enemy. Nothing softened him and Ana was allowed no spirit. I fought my way out of things but she could not. She was a girl and suffered for it. Time will tell if she can regain her sight. I do not know what will happen now. When she has somewhat recovered I will take her back to the specialists although you have done more than any psychiatrist she has seen.'

'Guilt like that is hard to confess,' Maggie said softly.

'She confessed to you.' He looked at her and smiled ruefully. 'She would probably have told Mitchell sooner or later.'

'Later, I think,' Maggie said in amusement. 'However, the turmoil of Mitch going helped to bring it all out.'

'So everything was for the best, Maggie?'

She shrugged and turned away. It was not the best for her.

'Maggie!' He reached out for her and pulled her into his arms, looking down at her, his hand against her face. 'Be close to me. I need you close,' he breathed huskily, pulling her closer.

'There's a lot of difference. . .'

He lifted her face, his lips moving over her skin hungrily, and the sensuous pleasure was there at once with no need at all for him to arouse her. She arched against him with a wantonness she was completely unaware of and his voice was thick with desire as he whispered against her ear.

'What difference, Maggie? We are both heated by the same fire. Sometimes you are fierce and angry but it is all a cover for the soft innocence inside you. I would never hurt you. There is no need for any defence with me.' His teeth nipped at her ear, sending sensation spiralling through her and Maggie sagged against him.

He tightened her to him, parting her lips, and she moaned at the primitive caress of his tongue stroking against hers, exploring her mouth. She could feel her own heart pounding against her ribs and there was a passionate urgency inside her that robbed her of all thought. It was like swimming in warm darkness, only her slender arms around his neck holding her upright as his hands caressed her body and moulded her against him.

They had been close like this before but not at Felipe's instigation. In the past she had shamelessly melted towards him and he had accepted her, only to put her aside later. The thought crept into the warmth and she trembled, afraid that this time she could not face rejection.

'What is it?' Instantly he felt her change of mood. His hands came back to close tightly around her face. 'Tell me, Maggie.'

'This time if you leave me I can't. . .'

'Neither can I,' he said thickly. 'I know what you need, *querida*. I need it too.' He placed heated kisses along the slender line of her neck, arching her against him until the path of his lips reached the warm, scented valley between her breasts. 'I cannot walk away unless you ask me to go.'

She sighed and relaxed and when his lips sought hers again she met them with matching urgency. He poured out so much passion that she melted against him, completely willing, enslaved, and his hand moved impatiently to the zip of her dress, moving it down until the cool night air on her skin made her shiver.

'You will not be cold for long, *querida*.' The slurred sound of his voice told her that he was as committed to this as she was herself and there would be no drawing back, no leaving her. He pushed the dress free and lifted her into his arms, walking to the bed, and Maggie made a small whimpering noise she didn't even recognise, a softly feminine noise of submission.

'Don't be afraid, Maggie. I know how you feel.' The strain in his voice made her realise how much he still held his emotions on a tight rein and his dark eyes roamed over her hungrily as he undressed in the soft lamplight. For a second his eyes met hers and then he came to her quickly, his body covering her own, pressing her down into the softness of the bed, his skin against hers an almost unbearable pleasure.

'You have never felt this before?' His hand moved down the length of her body, stroking away her remaining garments, his eyes watching her as she shivered with delight, shaking her head wildly, and he bent his head, a growl of satisfaction leaving his throat in a completely masculine way. This time, though, Maggie did not resent the male domination. This was the man she would follow if he merely smiled. He would not even have to snap his fingers.

She responded wildly as he caressed her and it drove him further along the path of passion. His earlier gentleness drained away swiftly until his hands were heated, his mouth fierce as he claimed her breasts, and her wild cries only served to increase his demands until she was shaking in his arms.

'Now, Maggie!' She felt his body surge against her own and instinctively she softened, meeting the fierce possession with no fear at all. He gasped her name as her body closed around him and then she was dominated by his power until she slid off the end of the world into warm darkness.

She had no idea how exhausted she would be, how lethargic, and she opened her eyes slowly to find him watching her, his breathing still ragged. There were tears on her cheeks and he carefully eased them away with gentle fingers.

'I hurt you? In the heat of the moment I forgot that you were so innocent.' He smiled wryly, his dark glance sweeping over her face. 'You made me forget, my sensuous little cat.' He moved away and pulled her into his arms, his hands beginning to soothe and caress her gently. 'You imagine I will still let you go back to

London?' he asked huskily. 'We have now reached the time when you become lost in the mountains until they forget you.'

'You know I'll have to go,' Maggie said tremulously, not yet back to earth, her body still shivering with delight and reaction.

'I know only what I want. I need you and you need me.'

His arms held her tightly but Maggie felt the cold wave of reality and shivered. She knew now how much she loved him and with Felipe it was all desire. It had seemed right, not important to be his forever. She had imagined she could face his passion and then remember it with warmth. She had not realised how she would never stop needing him but now she could see the future and it was dark.

His hands swept over her and she curled against him willingly in spite of her fears, bringing back that same quickening of his breath. She might lose him but for now he was as enslaved as she was and Maggie caressed him as he caressed her until his kisses grew more demanding and he turned her beneath him again.

His lips burned her. He slowly kissed every part of her and suddenly he stopped, his hand running gently over her thigh, his uneven breathing easing as he explored her skin.

'Maggie? What is this?' He was looking at the scar that ran from her hip almost to her knee. There was nothing unpleasant about it, as she knew quite well, but it brought Maggie out of the renewed clouds of desire.

'An accident.' Even her voice was different and he came up on one elbow to look into her face, seeing all the fire die out of her.

'What sort of accident?' His dark eyes held hers but she tore her gaze away. Now she was embarrassed, shy, and he seemed to know it. He covered them both with the cool sheets but he had no intention of giving up his questioning. When she turned her head away he captured her face between strong hands and made her look at him.

'What sort of accident?' he demanded.

'Just—just an accident. I'm sorry. I know it looks bad.'

'It does not and you know that perfectly well. It is a neat white scar. You are beautiful all over, desirable, and it was not an accident. It was an operation.'

'Well, yes. But—but I was in an accident and. . .'

'Maggie!' His hands held her face tightly and she met his gaze at last, her lip caught between her teeth.

'It was two men. They attacked me.' She wanted to get it out, get it over and done with, and she could not have said anything worse.

'*Dios!* You have suffered this violence? That is why you freeze over and protect yourself. You let me make love to you fiercely, you have given yourself to me when you have good cause to hate men!'

'It wasn't like that,' she protested shakily. 'It wasn't what you think. It was just mindless, senseless violence. It was when I first went to London. I don't have any family. When my grandfather died there was no one. I was working on a different magazine then. I had a flat and a job but no friends. I hadn't been there long enough. I was going back to my flat one evening and I had no cause to feel unsafe. The streetlights were on and I was almost there.

'Two men sprang out at me from the little park. They wanted my bag and they grabbed it, but then they started to beat me for no reason except sheer wickedness. I screamed and fought but nobody came. Finally they—they tired of it and ran off. A man and woman passed and they got an ambulance. I was quite badly injured, especially my leg. When I got out of hospital I dared not go outside. I had new locks fitted and—and I just stayed there. A girl from the magazine used to do my shopping and in the end I managed to do it myself, going by taxi and feeling terrified all the time.'

She stopped and Felipe held her close, his hand stroking her hair.

'How did you survive, my brave, beautiful Maggie?' he asked gently.

'By hatred. In the end I asked myself why I should be trapped in there while they walked about freely. I started drawing them as well as I could remember. Then I destroyed them, sometimes tearing them into little strips, sometimes burning them. I made them suffer and gradually the fear went, but it left a—a sort of boiling rage.'

'Towards all men,' he asked quietly.

'Yes. Mitch somehow got around me. I suppose I was stuck with him, like it or not. Anyway, it all gave me a lot of confidence. I applied for a job on *Query* and got it. I did so well because I was hard.'

'Not hard, Maggie,' he corrected softly, 'merely injured inside.' He looked deeply into her eyes. 'And tonight? Are you injured again?'

'No. I'm whole, cured. You've been changing me since I came to Spain.' She buried her face against him, afraid to say any more in case he guessed how she felt, and he gathered her close, reaching out to switch off the lamps.

'Go to sleep, *querida*,' he said softly. 'You are completely safe.'

'Are you going to your room?' Maggie asked in a whisper, longing for him to stay.

'Of course not. If I go I will only take you with me and this bed is already warm. You can go to sleep. I know you are worn out. I have some thinking to do.'

'What about?' Maggie curled against him and yawned drowsily, her head against his shoulder. It felt so right, as if she really belonged there, and she heard his dark laughter.

'About you, Maggie Howard. At this moment I can think of nothing else.'

# CHAPTER TEN

FELIPE was gone when she woke up next morning and Maggie felt a great burst of anxiety. She had no idea how to act now, how to face him. Ana was having breakfast when she went downstairs and Maggie spoke softly to her.

'How do you feel?'

'A little shocked still. Oh, Maggie, I'm sorry I blamed you for telling Felipe. I would never have told him myself.'

'Has it helped, though?' Maggie was relieved to see the old smile back on Ana's face and glad at this moment that Felipe wasn't there.

'Yes. Felipe sat with me for a long time. He explained so much that I had not known. My father made no attempt ever to control his rages even though he knew his condition. I didn't know at all.'

'So you've got no guilt now?' Maggie asked.

'No. Thanks to you, Maggie.' Ana suddenly frowned. 'I was going to be happy today, really happy. I was going to get you to talk about Mitch and England but now it is impossible.'

'Why is it?' Maggie said with a laugh. 'I'm always ready to talk.'

'I think you'll change your mind,' Ana muttered. 'Felipe is out there with the Rainfords. They arrived a little while ago. I don't know how long they're staying but when they come here it is usually impossible to get rid of them.'

The laughter died on Maggie's face. She felt utterly defenceless. She could still feel Felipe's arm around her, her body felt the force of his passion, and now he was out there with a woman who behaved as if he was her

166

personal possession. For the first time in two years, Maggie simply wanted to run. How could she face him now?

He solved her problem because when he came in with a very satisfied-looking Candace Rainford beside him he came straight over to Maggie.

'You slept late.' He stood behind her chair and smiled down into her upturned face. When she just nodded shyly his hands came to her shoulders, warm, possessive hands that stayed right there for the two visitors to see. 'We have company for the day,' he added, and Candace pouted coyly.

'We usually stay longer than a day, Felipe,' she murmured, her eyes on the hands that soothed Maggie's shoulders.

'Normally you are welcome to stay for as long as you like,' he said quietly. 'This time, though, you have walked into what must be a time of private family discussion.'

'Miss Howard is here,' Candace pointed out a little shrilly.

'She has been here a long time and will be here for even longer,' Felipe answered smoothly. 'I really do not think I could manage my affairs without her assistance.'

Maggie's face was glowing pink and she was glad that Ana could not see her. She could see Ana, though, and the face that had drooped at the idea of these visitors was now having great difficulty in not breaking into wide smiles.

Later in the hall, Maggie tackled Felipe.

'Did you have to be like that?' she asked crossly. 'That woman clearly thinks we—we. . .'

'Thinks we are lovers?' he enquired helpfully. 'We are, *paloma*.'

'If it's just to stop her from clinging round your neck. . .'

'She does not,' he assured her silkily. 'I reserve that pleasure for you.' He caught her towards him and kissed her until she was breathless, and even in her daze she heard Candace's high heels clicking angrily across the back of the hall. Felipe heard it too and he raised his head, smiling down into Maggie's flushed face.

'Now she is sure that we are lovers.' His fist pushed playfully against her chin and then he walked off laughing, leaving her once again trembling and defence-less. She had no idea how he felt now.

They had to entertain the visitors and Felipe would not let Maggie slide out of it. It seemed that for reasons of his own he wanted to make quite sure that the woman knew how things stood, and really she could not have been left in any doubt, Maggie thought. He had hardly left her side, and even Ana knew. It clearly pleased Ana but pleasure was the last thing Candace felt. Jealousy was wildly in her eyes but if Felipe noticed he chose to ignore it.

One good thing came from it. Felipe's possessive attitude rid her of the attentions of Peter Rainford and when Felipe offered to show them Ana's skills neither of them looked overjoyed.

'It will be the first time she has had an outside audience,' he said crisply. 'It will be good for her.'

'Is she ready for a public performance?' Candace asked Maggie peevishly as Felipe went to saddle the horse. 'I expect you've watched her.'

'Many times,' Ana sang out, her hand sliding into Maggie's arm, 'but of course Maggie is not an outsider. Therefore, I would value your comments.'

Maggie almost cringed at the outright challenge but Candace said nothing at all. Apparently, though, it was all too much for her husband — he left very quietly. He was not at all interested in this display of equestrian skill and he probably knew to get clear of his wife when her temper was roused.

In spite of the gathering clouds of rage, however, once again Ana held Maggie spellbound. With the guilt swept from her mind, Ana seemed to have improved almost overnight and the pleasure on Felipe's face told Maggie that he saw it too. They were both spellbound.

Jorge appeared in the open doorway and attracted Felipe's attention.

'*Teléfono, señor*,' he said urgently. 'It is from Inglaterra, Señor Parnham.'

Maggie saw Felipe's face tighten.

'Keep practising,' he called to Ana. 'If Devlin imagines he is calling you back,' he muttered as he passed Maggie, 'he is about to be corrected.' He walked out into the bright sunlight and Maggie turned back to Ana. She was doing those fantastic leaps, her mind utterly taken with it, a joy to watch, and when Candace Rainford gripped Maggie's arm she was quite taken by surprise.

'You think you're clever, don't you?' she spat. 'What are you after all but a journalist? I expect you imagine you'll be a countess soon?'

Maggie was stunned, but not for long; her temper surfaced.

'Mind your own business!' she said clearly. 'What Felipe and I decide has nothing to do with you.'

'Nothing to do with me? He had plenty to do with me before you came, flashing your eyes at him!'

'You're married!' Maggie said in disgust, her heart sinking.

'It never worried him,' Candace said scathingly.

Maggie had forgotten that, Ana being blind, her hearing was acute, and the horse was upon them before she realised it.

'How dare you?' Ana shouted. 'How dare you say such things about Felipe?'

'What do you know, you stupid girl? You can't even see!' Candace was enraged. She lashed out, her arm swinging wildly. Maggie stepped aside but the horse, already alarmed at the shouting, reared high and Ana, too incensed at the attack on Felipe's honour, was completely off guard. She fell heavily and the raised hoof caught Maggie on the shoulder so powerfully that she too fell, pain washing over her like fire. She tried to get to Ana but fainted as she moved.

When Maggie woke up she was in bed, the hacienda silent, the room lit by one soft lamp, and Felipe was sitting in a chair by the bed.

'Felipe?' At the sound of her voice he came to her quickly, taking her hand.

'It's all right. I gave you a sedative. You're very bruised and you were shaking badly.'

'Ana?' Maggie struggled to get up, gasping with pain and clutching his arm, but his warm fingers closed round hers.

'Keep still. She is fine. I took her to Jaén and they are keeping her in hospital until tomorrow at the very least. She banged her head badly.'

'She was angry and off guard. The horse reared,' Maggie said miserably, sinking back to the pillows as she remembered what Candace had said, and he nodded seriously.

'I know. She told me when she came round.' He looked at her intently. 'It is not true, Maggie. I have never had an affair with that woman. Her husband was always with us but as a couple they were difficult to dislodge without rudeness. It is not the Spanish habit to order people out when they visit—not until today,' he added grimly.

Maggie looked so glad that he took her hand and raised it to his lips, kissing each finger as his eyes held hers.

'Maggie, Ana can see,' he murmured softly. 'You eased her mind and the blow she took as she fell did the rest. You have completed your task. You have brought happiness to a house where it has never really been before. The Hacienda de Nieve is a different place because of you.'

'She can see?' Tears came to Maggie's eyes. A tremendous happiness filled her and her hand came out to touch his face. 'Strangely, things work out for the best,' she whispered.

'With you they seem to,' he murmured gently, his dark eyes holding hers.

'Will Ana be all right?'

'So they say, and I believe them. She was in good spirits when I left. She did not even seem to mind the rather bad headache. She sent you her love.'

'Stay with me,' Maggie said without any thought at all, just with a great desire to be able to be near him.

'I intend to sit by you all night. I have been here since I came from the hospital and while I was there Maria sat by you. Go to sleep, Maggie; I'll be here.'

Maggie smiled and he bent his dark head and kissed her, holding her hand and simply letting her fall asleep.

Maggie drove home from the office. She hadn't got free until nearly seven and by the time she had negotiated the traffic and turned towards her flat it was eight o'clock. She was feeling pleased, almost triumphant. Her article had quite astounded Richie because it was like nothing she had done before.

'What did you think of the shots? Fabulous, aren't they?' Maggie had asked brightly.

'Fabulous!' he had growled sarcastically. Since Maggie had returned, suspicion had been etched across Richie's face every day, and it was there now. Mitchell had refused to hand over his prints from Spain until Maggie came back. Now they had suddenly appeared and Mitchell wasn't even in the country.

'You've got to admit it's all good. Good, glossy stuff.'

'Good? Glossy? Maybe,' he admitted grudgingly, his black scowl deepening. 'I don't expect things to be just good when you do them, however. I expect amazing revelations — a scoop!'

'If you wanted that you shouldn't have sent me somewhere tame,' Maggie pointed out, nearly laughing

as she said the word. Tame! It had been anything but
tame. 'There was no scoop material, just beauty, peace
and astonishing skill. It's all there and Mitch's shots are
fantastic, plenty to choose from. As to a scoop, just hold
the article back for a while and I think you'll have one.
That girl's going to be a sensation—just as her brother
was.'

She fixed her grey eyes on him and he gave in. After
all, the article was excellent and she was probably right;
she usually was. The shots were brilliant and he wasn't
too sure about Maggie. She looked different somehow
and she might just be up to something. She was as
bright as a button. If he hadn't known that fact himself,
Devlin Parnham had pointed it out to him repeatedly
with a self-satisfied little smirk. Richie had the feeling
that something had escaped his attention.

Maggie knew all about his qualms. Devlin Parnham
was a scheming man and there was little chance of
Richie's being informed of Maggie's exact mission to
Spain. It had amused her all the way through the heavy
traffic, but now her thoughts went far away, back with
Felipe. Her thoughts were always there.

She had written about a brilliant girl who in spite of
two years of blindness would one day represent Spain
as her illustrious brother had done. She had written
about the beauty of Andalucía, about the soaring mountains, about the great hacienda where Ana trained. She
had written about Felipe and his genius and she was
very pleased with the way she had ended her article.

One day, very soon, the name of Santis will once
again bring pleasure and astonishment to everyone.
Once again there will be a 'Magnificent' de Santis,
but this time it will be a very beautiful young woman
called Ana.

As for Felipe, he had not asked her to stay in Spain
with him. She had decided to come back to her job.
There was no way she would demand anything from

him. Loving him had made her whole again. She had seen Ana and then left as soon as she could. Felipe merely wanted her, not a lasting emotion. There was her article to write and her whole way of life in London. They were worlds apart and she knew it as much as he did. She would go on loving him but she would not disrupt his life further.

In any case, Felipe had said nothing. Not by even one sign had he shown that he wanted her to stay in any capacity at all. He too recognised the great gap that yawned between them. He had kissed her goodbye and seen her on to her flight. She had solved his problem with Ana, belonged to him, and he had looked at her deeply with a great deal of affection.

'I still want to see that article, Maggie Howard,' he had teased. 'I've changed my mind. I approve every word or I'll sue your magazine.'

He had held on to her hand as her flight was called, and it had given her the way out without tears.

'You still want the bun and the biscuit?' she had mocked.

'Of course.' He'd kissed her hand and then she was gone. No tears, no fuss, no hurt showing. Maggie Howard at her best.

It hurt now, though. Living without Felipe was lonely, hard, and the city did really seem to be grey and cold even though the days were warm and long. She saw his face in everyone, went to sleep with thoughts of him in her mind, dreamed of him and awoke with tears on her cheeks. She had sent the article and included a note to Ana, but although Ana had written enthusiastically Felipe had not even sent his kind regards.

She pulled herself up sharply, realising that tears were threatening right now and she wasn't even home yet. She never let herself slip like that. It was just that things were getting worse, not better as time passed. By the time she turned into the long street to her flat, however, she had herself under control.

And luckily too. Her eyebrows rose in astonishment when she saw that somebody had taken her parking place. There was limited space here and only residents were allowed to park. They all had permits and the rules were strictly adhered to with a heavy fine for intruders. Now, a great black car with tinted windows was taking up not only her place but part of the next place too. She managed to manoeuvre into the remaining space and got out to give somebody a piece of her mind.

The traffic was too heavy for her to go to the driver's side and she stormed along the pavement to the offending car and opened the passenger door.

'You're not allowed to park here,' she began heatedly. 'This place is mine.'

A long arm shot out and before she could scream or struggle she was pulled into the car and into strong arms.

'I am allowed to do whatever I want,' Felipe assured her determinedly. His eyes went to her head and he snatched her hat free and flung it into the back of the car. '*Cielos*! Take that damned hat off!' His eyes flared over her astonished face. 'I see we have no legs again, Señorita Howard. We are back to trousers, hats and no hair at all.'

'Why are you here?' Maggie asked breathlessly, sitting wide-eyed and making no move to stop him when his hands went to her hair and pulled it free of the restraining band. She couldn't believe it. This had to be some wonderful dream, because Felipe de Santis would not come here to England and seek her out.

He watched the glorious hair cascade around her and then his dark eyes held hers.

'Why am I here? Can you manage without me?' he asked softly.

'No.' Maggie could only whisper and his eyes continued to look very serious.

'Then surely that answers your question? I am here

because you cannot manage without me, and I know it.'
His hand cupped her face possessively as he drew her
towards him. 'You will freeze up again, become fierce
and forget how to be alive.' His lips brushed hers. 'I
cannot manage without you either and I've given you
all the time I intend to,' he whispered against her
mouth. 'I am here because you belong to me.' His lips
closed over hers and Maggie sank into the bliss of the
only domination she would ever accept.

They were hungry for each other and Maggie surren-
dered to the fierce possession of his mouth. They might
have been alone in the mountains, because the passing
traffic never even penetrated their minds. There was
just feeling, wild and deep, intense pleasure that even
bordered on pain, and Maggie's head was on his
shoulder, her eyes locked with his when he at last raised
his head and looked down at her bewitched face.

'My sensuous innocent,' he said thickly. 'I have been
going out of my mind thinking about you.'

'Oh, Felipe!'

'Oh, Maggie!' he mocked huskily. 'Did you imagine
even for one moment that I would let you go?'

'Why did you?' She was mesmerised by the intense,
dark eyes and he stroked her flushed face, before
tangling his fingers in her shining hair.

'Many reasons. But mostly because I wanted you to
have time to make comparisons. I wanted you to be
able to make up your mind away from the pull of the
mountains, the sunshine and the hacienda. I made you
live again and I wanted to know there was more than
mere excitement for you.'

'You gave me so much,' Maggie whispered.

'And you gave me everything, my beautiful Maggie.
The trouble is, I want everything for a very long
time—forever.' He pulled her closer, his lips brushing
her again. 'Come with me, Maggie!'

Once again his mouth possessed hers and Maggie's
heart threatened to beat right out of her body. He was

here! He had come for her! She had no idea what he
intended, but whatever it was she would go with Felipe
wherever he led.

'How did you know where I lived?' Maggie asked as she
was once again in the car and being driven away from
her flat.

'The address was on the note you sent to Ana,' he
reminded her. 'I observed that there was no letter for
me.'

'I — I didn't think you'd want. . .'

'I want,' he murmured, his dark gaze lancing over
her. 'I want all the time.' He relented when she blushed
and looked as if she was about to start trembling. 'Also
there was Mitch. He drew me a small but accurate
map.'

'Mitch?' Maggie's head shot up and she stared at him
in astonishment. 'He's in Germany!'

'He is in London,' Felipe corrected. 'He came back
this morning but his journey was long. A detour to
Spain was apparently necessary. At this moment he will
be getting ready to take Ana out for a meal and the
theatre, then he will be escorting her back to her hotel —
and Maria.'

'You brought Maria?'

'Naturally. I could not do two things at once. I did
not intend to spend my time being a chaperon for my
sister. I came for you.'

'Where are we going?' Maggie asked breathlessly.

'To my hotel. I have ordered dinner for two in my
suite.'

'Can I have a chaperon?' Maggie asked mockingly,
fighting hard to stop her legs from trembling.

'No!' He never said anything else and after a minute
Maggie got her breath back and asked,

'Why — why did I have to pack a bag just for dinner
when. . .?'

'You will not be coming back,' he assured her in the

same arrogant tone. 'Tomorrow we will look for a house
to rent but as I only arrived in London this morning I
have not had the time. When we get a house we will
collect all your things.'

It silenced Maggie completely. She didn't know what
to say at all. They were going to rent a house and she
was going to live with him. She already knew that she
would but inside she felt a great hurt begin to grow. He
still knew how far apart they were. For Felipe it was just
desire after all.

It was the same splendid hotel, even the same suite,
and Maggie put her bag down as Felipe locked the door.
She walked into the sumptuously furnished sitting-room
feeling lost and not a little frightened.

'Are — are we staying here?'

'I have already said so. I have ordered dinner but it
will not be served for another hour. Would you like a
drink?'

She could only shake her head. Since she had got into
the car with him to come here he had become still and
watchful — worrying. She was so aware of him that he
seemed to be touching her from a long way off. Her
whole body seemed to be listening for him. If she had to
leave him again she didn't know what she would do.

'You — you want me to — to live with you, Felipe?' she
asked in little more than a whisper.

'It is normal,' he assured her. He was much closer
than she had anticipated and his arms came round her
from behind, circling her waist and pulling her back
against him. 'Stop being afraid, Maggie,' he said softly.
His hand brushed aside the long, thick hair, his lips
beginning to move over her tender nape, and Maggie
gave a small whimper of desire, melting against him.

'Maggie!' His hand moved to tug her shirt free of the
waistband of her trousers and she felt his touch on the
warmth of her skin, his fingers moulding her body like a
contented tiger. When his hands cupped her swollen

breasts she tilted her head back willingly, her mouth already open as he bent his dark head to hers.

'Felipe!' She moaned his name and he swept her into his arms, moving through into the lamplit bedroom and undressing her quickly. Maggie was undressing him impatiently too although she had no real idea of what she was doing. She wound her arms around his neck, eagerly accepting his heated kisses until he lifted her on to the bed and came down on top of her, covering her and dominating her.

His hands cupped her face as he moved over her sensuously and Maggie moved beneath him, her breath a wild gasping sound that brought more pressure from the sleek, demanding body.

'I want your magic in my arms, your head on my pillow,' he murmured thickly into her mouth. 'I want to own you utterly, possess your soul, give you my children. You're mine!'

His sensuous words intoxicated her, the heated darkness of his eyes intoxicated her, and Maggie gave a sharp, bewitched cry as he suddenly possessed her, coming deeply into her, his mouth cutting off any further cry as he made a low, dark sound deep in his throat and arched her beneath him.

'My woman,' he muttered huskily. 'You were always my woman from the moment I saw you.' He raised his head and looked down at her fiercely, holding her tightly against him. 'Tell me you love me,' he demanded. 'Tell me!'

'I love you, Felipe!' She could only whisper the words, her feelings were too intense, and his lips covered hers as he held her head to his and began to move inside her. The soaring excitement grew until they were both unaware of any world at all. Maggie only knew that their bodies were locked together, belonging, draining each other of all feeling and power. When the end came, Maggie gave a low, shaken moan and collapsed beneath him, her feelings so deep that she began to cry, soft, uncontrollable sobbing that brought his arms around her and his lips to her heated face.

'Maggie!' When she looked at him through eyes swimming with tears his face was taut with feeling, his eyes filled with burning tenderness. '*Querida!*' he said thickly. 'I love you. Marry me.'

'Marry you?' She looked up at him with enormous grey eyes, tears still streaming down her cheeks.

'Yes.' His lips began to gather her tears, moving over her eyes and her soft cheeks. 'I can't live without you, *mi amor,*' he said simply.

It was very late when they finally had the meal that Felipe had ordered, and they were still in each other's arms, talking and planning, when dawn began to break.

'Come home with me, *dulce amor,*' Felipe begged softly, stroking back the dark red hair from her face. 'Come back to the mountains. You can write there, do anything you wish. You will make the place happy as you did before.'

'I don't ever want to be away from you again,' Maggie confessed, winding her arms around his neck. 'I'll write but I might be very busy having those children you want.'

The teasing words brought instant and delicious reprisals, and later Felipe sighed and leaned back, holding her in his arms.

'You will be very busy,' he warned. 'Ana needs a very strong-willed sister-in-law. Now that she can see again she is proving to be a handful of trouble.'

'You need a tough English lady to cope with her?' Maggie asked mockingly.

'You coped with me,' he retorted, smiling down at her. 'Ana will be easier but with Mitch arriving every other weekend you may have to lay down the law a little.'

'She'll be all right,' Maggie assured him softly. 'What about her training? I've already written about it. I'm not going to let her slide out of it or I don't get my scoop.'

'No chance of her sliding out of it,' he grinned, 'unless her teacher is too busy with his wife.'

Ana did not slide out of things. A year later Maggie sat with her husband and waited with rising excitement as the announcement was made to the vast crowds at Wembley.

'And now, the new hope of Spain, a wonder and a joy to watch. Ladies and gentlemen, Señorita Ana de Santis!'

Maggie gripped Felipe's hand as Ana rode into the arena on her white horse. Dressed in black with a white shirt, her blue-black hair severely braided under a black Córdoba hat, she was the very image of the brother whom Maggie had seen and dreamed of so long ago. The haughty looks were there, no sign of the mischievous girl she had become, and as she performed Maggie's eyes slid to her husband's face, seeing the pride and pleasure there.

'She is good, *querida*?' he whispered, feeling her eyes on him.

'Almost as good as you, darling.' He took her hand and held it tenderly and they both smiled as Mitch at Maggie's side muttered,

'Come on, baby! You can do it!'

She could. Her performance brought the house down and as they stood to go back and see her Maggie suddenly realised that Mitch was no longer there.

'He beat us to it,' she informed Felipe crossly as he guided her through the crowd, protecting her from knocks. 'How typical! You should have been allowed to congratulate her first. You put all the work in.'

'Don't fret, my love,' Felipe urged, smiling down at her. 'It is only natural. He loves her.'

'Well I never!' Maggie said mockingly. 'Who would have thought it?'

'Teasing always brings reprisals,' he murmured seductively, his arm coming round her. 'I believe you do it deliberately in order to be punished.'

Maggie blushed like a rose. She couldn't live without the sort of punishment that Felipe thought appropriate. She was still flustered when they found Ana and Mitch. They were hugging each other and Ana broke free to come and kiss both of them, her arms hugging Maggie carefully.

'Maggie! You managed to come. It was a bit risky surely?'

'Not too risky,' Maggie smiled. 'I feel fine and in any case I wanted to be here in person and not have to watch you on television. I told the baby to wait.'

'And he has waited long enough,' Felipe said, looking down at Maggie. 'I'll get you home now. However appropriate, we can't have our baby born with horses stamping all round.'

'Come and have dinner with us,' Maggie invited, looking at Mitch and at Ana's glowing face. 'It might be my last chance to entertain you for some time to come.'

They had bought a house in London so that for some time each year they could be in England, and now, with the baby almost due, Felipe had brought Maggie back.

'Well,' Mitch said with a considering look, 'normally I would say we wanted to be alone tonight, but as I'm going to be an uncle very soon. . .'

'An uncle?' Maggie stared at him and Ana held out her hand, allowing them to see the glittering ring at last.

'I am engaged,' she announced happily.

'Er — so am I,' Mitch added with a grin.

'We'll break out the champagne,' Felipe promised when the congratulations were over. 'I have to get Maggie home now. Don't be too long. She has to get plenty of rest. Too much excitement is bad for her.'

'I thrive on excitement!' Maggie protested as she was led firmly away.

'Only one type of excitement at the moment, *paloma*,' he murmured, smiling down into her annoyed face. 'Besides, if we hurry home, I can have you all to myself for a while before they come.'

'In that case,' Maggie said happily, snuggling against him as he put her in the car and came to sit beside her, 'I won't argue.'

'Of course you will not,' he informed her imperiously. 'I have tamed you. But do not be too tamed,' he added, pulling her into his arms. 'It is something I love to work at.'

He suddenly stopped teasing and looked down at her lovely face as she rested against his shoulder.

'I love you, Maggie de Santis,' he said deeply. 'I do not want to share you with anyone at all.' His hand rested warmly against the swollen mound of her stomach. 'I do not even want to share you with him.'

'You'll never have to share me,' Maggie whispered as his lips hovered over her own. 'It's a different kind of love—love we'll both be giving.' Her hand gently stroked his dark, determined face. 'This kind of love we'll keep for ourselves.'

'*Siempre*,' he promised as his lips met hers. 'Always, *mi amor*.'

## ANDALUCÍA

An amalgam by name, an amalgam by nature — that's Andalucía in a nutshell! For it owes its name to a mixture of Arabic words meaning 'Vandal's house', and also combines all that we have come to associate with Spain — from castanets to whitewashed *casas*, bullfights to beaches. The region has it all, so you are guaranteed not to be disappointed, and wherever you are you will have the opportunity to bask in the sun and the culture.

## THE ROMANTIC PAST

Andalucía is the birthplace of modern bullfighting *á pie*, having been invented by Pedro Romero, who was the first to use the modern *muleta* (red cape).

One of Córdoba's treasures is the **Medina Azahara**, built in the 10th century by Abderraman III for his favourite wife Azahara. He surrounded the palace with almond groves so that in the spring, when they turned white, Azahara would be reminded of the snow she loved to see in the Sierra Nevada when she lived in Granada.

Sevilla is the city that inspired such masterpieces as *Carmen*, *Don Giovanni*, and *The Barber of Seville*.

**Hemingway**, German poet **Rainer Marie Rilke** and **Orson Welles** were regular visitors to Ronda, the latter's ashes having been buried just outside the town.

**THE ROMANTIC PRESENT** — pastimes for lovers. . .

Since Andalucía covers an area of 34,000 square miles, it is unlikely that you will be able to see it all on one trip, but to give you a taste of what the region as a whole has to offer here's a selection of 'highlights' to steer you in the right direction. . .

Firstly, no trip to Andalucía would be complete without a visit to Sevilla — a truly romantic city where you will be charmed by the exotic parks and typically Spanish whitewashed buildings. Widely regarded as the centre of Andalusian culture and the Spanish Renaissance, Sevilla has plenty to see, including the third largest cathedral in the world and the largest Gothic edifice ever built. The impressive 14th century **Alcázar** is the residence of Juan Carlos whenever he visits the city, and is the oldest palace still used by royalty. In the new part of the city you can wander around the lovely gardens and courtyards of the **Parque de María Luisa** or hire a boat in the park alongside the **Plaza de España** and take a romantic row on the miniature canal. Also make time for **Barrio de Triana**, which used to be a separate village but is now part of the city. It's an ideal place to have a snack at one of the several *tapas* bars, and if you are there in the evening you can enjoy the gorgeous sunset along the river.

One of the liveliest provincial capitals in the region is
**Granada**, whose centre **Plaza Nueva** boasts some fine
Renaissance architecture. The fortifications of the
Moorish Alhambra are also well worth seeing, and
comprises four main areas: the **Alcázar** (royal palace);
the **Generalife** (summer palace); the splendid **Palacio
de Carlos V** — built by Pedro Machura, who was a
pupil of Michelangelo, and widely considered the most
beautiful Renaissance building in Spain; and the Alcazaba, which is the oldest part of the fortress. If you
climb the watchtower of the Alcazaba you will enjoy the
best view of Granada and the Sierra Nevada.

For more stunning views don't forget **Ronda**, a city split
into two halves by an earthquake and connected by
three bridges — a Moorish, Roman and so-called 'new
bridge', which was built in 1735. Ronda is worth the
trip just to see the amazing sight of the precipitous gorge
carved out by the Guadalevín River, and there is a
lovely park that is home to canaries, doves, ducks and
swans, pretty gardens and a water fountain.

If you are not afraid of the dark, and are interested in
prehistoric caves, you can visit either the three ancient
**dolmen** caves at Antequera — the oldest and best
preserved prehistoric tombs in Europe, or the subter-
ranean museum **Cuevas de la Pileta**, which contains
fascinating cave paintings, bones and stalagmites and
stalactites.

For those of you who enjoy a glass of sherry, head for
**Jerez de la Frontera**, the place from which the drink
takes its English name. Here you can take a tour round
the wine cellars (*bodegas*) and sample the world's finest
sherry for free!

**Jaén** is one of only a few landlocked provinces in
Andalucía and is extremely fertile, producing wheat,

barley, hops and olive oil in abundance — this is the olive capital of Spain! Here you can enjoy breathtaking views of the surrounding mountains, and see fine examples of Andalusian architecture. This is an ideal place for romantic strolls in the sunshine among the olive groves. . .

In complete contrast the landscape of **Almería** bears close resemblance to the American western badlands. Why not visit **Mini-Hollywood** in **Tabernas** (about half an hour away from Almería)? Here you can wander through the streets of the film set which was built and used for numerous Clint Eastwood westerns, along with many other action films, and watch an impressively staged showdown!

No matter where you find yourself in Andalucía you will be able to sample some of the best of Spanish cuisine. For a lunchtime snack go to almost any bar or café and you will find many *tapas* on offer — the variety is huge, ranging from salamis and cubes of marinated beef to shrimp, whitebait, *patatas bravas* (potato chunks in a spicy sauce) and chunks of *tortilla*.

For dinner, seafood is excellent, especially in the area around Malaga. *Gazpacho*, a chilled soup, is a local speciality and *salmorejo* — a sauce version with hard boiled eggs — is delicious. *Rabo de Toro* (oxtail meat in a tomato sauce) is a Cordoban dish worth trying, and if you are in Granada for dinner try its *tortilla sacramonte* — a potato omelette filled with vegetables and ham (*tortillas* are omelettes in Spain!). Of course the rice-based dish *paella* will feature on almost every menu — it is often regarded as Spain's national dish, and is traditionally eaten at lunchtime. If you're not in a hurry, try *paella valenciana* (it takes at least twenty minutes to prepare!).

Almería is famous for its grapes, but, for those less calorie-conscious among you, why not try one of the light pastries shaped like a pie wedge called *Pastel Córdóbes*?

As for wines, Andalucía is famous for its sherry, of which there are three main types: *fino* (light, dry), *amontillado* (darker), and *oloroso* (sweet), but if you fancy a good table wine you might like to try a Rioja of which, again, there are several types. Or if you really need to quench your thirst there is an interesting variety of non-alcoholic drinks to choose from — try *horchata de almendra* (made with almonds) or *horchata de chufa* (sweet nut-based).

Andalusian nightlife is as frenetic or as sedate as you want to make it! If you are in Sevilla, the nightlife there is in full swing until seven or eight a.m. most nights — you can visit one of the many bars and discos, or see flamenco dancing at its best at Los Gallos, on the western side of Barrio Santa Cruz. But if you fancy a quieter evening, why not head for nearby Abades — once an 18th century mansion, now a bar, where you can enjoy a leisurely drink while listening to classical music?

Of course any one of the popular holiday resorts on the Costa del Sol or Costa de la Luz is a hive of activity in the evenings, and if your visit happens to coincide with the *Feria y Fiestas de San Bernabé* (June 9–17) in Marbella you will have the opportunity to watch bull-fights, fireworks and concerts. Alternatively, at Granada you can attend one of the open-air concerts at the palace of Carlo V any time from mid-June to early July, when the International Festival of Music and Dance is in progress. But for those of you who prefer a slower pace in more peaceful surroundings an evening in Ronda, sipping a drink while watching the stunning sunset from the *Puento Nuevo* (new stone bridge) cast red and orange light on the cliffs, is ideal. . .

## DID YOU KNOW THAT . . .?

\* Andalucía's exports include sherry and Seville oranges.

\* the Spanish currency is the peseta.

\* the Spanish for 'I love you' is '*Te amo*', *Te adoro*' or '*Te quiero*'!

POSTCARDS FROM EUROPE

HARLEQUIN PRESENTS®

Travel across Europe in 1994 with Harlequin Presents. Collect a new Postcards From Europe title each month!

Don't miss
**THE BRUGES ENGAGEMENT**
by Madeleine Ker
Harlequin Presents #1650

*Available in May, wherever Harlequin Presents books are sold.*

HPPFE5

Hi—

*I'm in trouble—I'm engaged to Stuart, but I suddenly wish my relationship with Jan Breydel wasn't strictly business. Perhaps it's simply the fairy-tale setting of Bruges. Belgium is such a romantic country!*

*Love, Geraldine*

## This June, Harlequin invites you to a wedding of

*Promised Brides*

Celebrate the joy and romance of weddings past with PROMISED BRIDES—a collection of original historical short stories, written by three best-selling historical authors:

*The Wedding of the Century*—MARY JO PUTNEY
*Jesse's Wife*—KRISTIN JAMES
*The Handfast*—JULIE TETEL

Three unforgettable heroines, three award-winning authors! PROMISED BRIDES is available in June wherever Harlequin Books are sold.

HARLEQUIN®

## Harlequin Books requests the pleasure of your company this June in Eternity, Massachusetts, for WEDDINGS, INC.

For generations, couples have been coming to Eternity, Massachusetts, to exchange wedding vows. Legend has it that those married in Eternity's chapel are destined for a lifetime of happiness. And the residents are more than willing to give the legend a hand.

Beginning in June, you can experience the legend of Eternity. Watch for one title per month, across all of the Harlequin series.

## HARLEQUIN BOOKS... NOT THE SAME OLD STORY!